Mother May I

Genevieve Jack

Carpe Luna Publishing

Mother May I: Knight Games series, Book 4

Copyright © 2015 Carpe Luna Publishing

Published by Carpe Luna, Ltd.,
PO Box 5932,
Bloomington, IL 61701
www.carpeluna.com

FIRST EDITION: MARCH 2015

ISBN: 978-1-940675-19-0

Cover design by Steven Novak

v 1.0

BOOKS BY GENEVIEVE JACK

Contents

CHAPTER 1
Return To Me

True wanting drains a soul. It's a persistent squeaky wheel at the back of your brain. I'd survived twenty-two years without Rick; a temporary hiatus from him should have been simple. But it wasn't. As I searched for him in the woods behind his cabin, following the metaphysical connection that lingered despite the loss of our emotional one, I ached with a need that bordered on obsession. He didn't remember me—no recollection at all of our shared history. But I remembered him. And that memory was a barb under my skin, a constant reminder that an evil witch had torn our love from its mooring and left us ruined.

Amid calls of songbirds, I broke from the trees to see the bright spring sun reflected on serene waters. Rick's silhouette was positioned on a fallen log near shore, broad shoulders hunched over a fishing pole in his hands. His caretaker powers meant he'd surely sensed me coming, and he turned to look at me

"I brought you something," I said, waiting to approach as if he were a skittish dog. My gift hung from my shoulder in a bag with the store's logo on the front. I kept it tucked under my elbow, nervous about how he'd perceive it.

Blessedly, Rick smiled and patted the section of the fallen log next to him. "Come." He rested his fishing pole on the ground between his feet.

"Fishing again?" I asked, lowering myself to the log next to him. I was not surprised, actually. Since Rick lost his memory, he'd taken to living the life he had before he became the vessel for my immortal soul, my caretaker. That life consisted mostly of fishing, hunting, and gardening. Harmless enough but a distraction from my goal of reviving his lost memory.

"Shhh." He held a finger to his lips. "You'll scare dinner."

"Wouldn't want to do that," I lied. In fact, I'd eaten more rabbit, venison, and freshwater fish of all kinds in the three weeks since he'd lost his memory than I had my entire life prior. The food wasn't bad. Rick could cook. He just couldn't enjoy it—not like I could, anyway. While Rick could eat, food wasn't nourishing to his constitution, nor did it taste any better than cardboard. Caretakers thrived on a diet of blood, sex, and supernatural souls. Although, since he lost his memory, Rick existed solely on my blood, served up in a glass that required no physical contact whatsoever.

"I was hoping you would come," he said. He leaned his elbows on his knees and turned toward me on the log. "You always loved fishing."

"You mean Isabella always loved fishing," I corrected. His gaze slipped from mine to a clump of moss near his feet. "If you're asking, I *like* fishing. I do. I went with my dad a few times. The lake was peaceful, and then there was the excitement of reeling in the catch. It was okay."

Rick turned his face toward me again, his eyes narrowing as if I were a puzzle to be solved. "What do you love, Grateful?"

The word *you* stuck in my throat. I rubbed my palms on my thighs. "I love taking care of people. That's why I became a nurse. I used to have a dog when I was little, and I would wrap up his leg with bandages and pretend he'd broken it. I'd feed him his food on a spoon, one nugget at a time."

He laughed. "Isabella also. She was a healer by nature. My father would go to her for peppermint elixir every time his stomach would ache. Everyone in town counted on her remedies."

Until they burned her, I wanted to finish for him. The wistful tone of his voice made a strange feeling come over me, and I stiffened. I was jealous. Jealous of myself in a previous life. This had to be a first.

"What did you bring?" he asked, gesturing toward the bag tucked protectively under my arm.

I maneuvered it onto my lap and pulled out the laptop computer I'd purchased for him. It was small and light, important features if, as I hoped, he'd bring it with him on excursions like this.

"What is it?"

I flipped the top open and logged in. "The password is hocus-pocus." I chuckled, but Rick stared at me blankly. "I thought it would be funny because I'm a witch."

He nodded but didn't laugh. I cleared my throat. "You can use the personal hotspot on your cell when you're out here." I helped myself to the phone in his jacket pocket and changed the settings.

The forlorn look on his face was a red flag of warning. Even with his memory intact, Rick never loved technology. Time to pull out the big guns. I placed the computer in his lap and moved to stand behind him. With some hesitation, I leaned over his shoulder and placed my hand on his. The chemical reaction from my touch was undeniable, his sharp inhale echoing mine. Where our skin touched felt hot, the starting point of a trail of electricity that meandered straight to my core. My cheek grazed his and I thought I might come undone.

Swallowing hard, I composed myself and helped him select the Internet icon. I clicked on the folder I'd made for this occasion and selected a video from the top of the list. My secret weapon: cat videos. The screen darkened for a moment. The clip started and a fluffball of a kitten pawed a roll of toilet paper, unraveling it faster and faster until it was up to its calico ears in a mound of quilted sheets.

Rick laughed under his breath.

I clicked another one. This video showed a kitten lying on its back in its owner's lap. The woman tickled its tummy and the cat curled into a ball, only to spread its paws wide when she stopped.

This time Rick laughed harder.

"It's not just for funny videos," I said softly into his ear as my chest brushed the back of his shoulder. "You can look up things on this, things about the world." I navigated to my favorite search engine. "Type what you want to know about, and it will show you a list of results."

I demonstrated by typing in *United States map* and clicking on the first result, which was an interactive atlas meant for elementary schoolers.

"This contraption has answers to everything?" he asked.

"Almost everything." I moved to click on New Hampshire.

The whir of the fishing reel sent Rick bounding off the log to lift the rod from its holder. Luckily, I caught the laptop as it slid from his lap. The absence of his body in front of me left me shivering in the cool spring air.

For Rick's part, he didn't seem to notice our disconnected bodies. He reeled and pulled back on the pole, which bent and wobbled from the force of the catch. When the fish was close enough, he waded into the water and scooped two fingers under the gills, lifting it from the lake.

"Bass," he said, proudly holding it so I could appreciate the magnificence of his catch.

"Way to go." Privately, I wondered where he'd store this latest catch. The freezer in his stone cottage was overflowing with wild game he would never eat.

"I imagine you are right. I have kept too many." He wrestled the hook from the fish's mouth and tossed his catch back into the water where it swam away in a flash.

"Rick… could you hear my thoughts just now?" Since his loss of memory, we still had our connection. At least, I could pick up on his thoughts. But it was oddly a one-way street. So far, he'd seemed oblivious to mine.

He looked at me for a second and shook his head. "Your face is a book easily read."

"I'm sorry. I just… I don't want it to go to waste." For a moment, the space between us seemed to grow even though neither of us took a step.

"You're right." He secured the line to his fishing pole and without another word, headed in the direction of his home, leaving the laptop and me behind.

Rattled, I plunged the computer back into its bag, slung it over my shoulder, and jogged to catch up with him. "Rick. You can still fish. You can put it in my freezer if you want." I didn't understand why he was so upset. Unless… Maybe he could hear my thoughts and just didn't want to admit it. Was he upset about the fish or that he had experienced more evidence of our connection?

"It's okay to be what you are," I called.

He stopped abruptly. "What exactly am I?"

"You're my caretaker." My voice cracked as I said it.

The desperate look he flashed broke my heart. "What, exactly, is the purpose of a caretaker?"

I hesitated. We'd talked about this before, but most of the time he rejected whatever I said. It was simply too much for his brain to absorb. Was he ready for more? "You take care of me."

"By feeding you my blood and protecting you when you're in danger," he said.

"Yes."

"In three weeks, I have not fed you my blood nor protected you from anything. If I am your caretaker, I am a failure. You seem to be doing quite well on your own." He turned on his heel and strode toward his stone cottage.

I picked up the pace, stomach tight. "Not as well as you might think."

He kept walking. Our connection was fuzzy, as if Rick was trying to block me but wasn't very good at it. He was upset; that much was obvious. The confusing part was why. Rick had always been an alpha male. To feel comfortable in his skin, he needed to play that role. Had I treated him too much like a patient and not enough like the man I knew he was? If so, to win him over, I needed to help him help me.

By the time we reached his place, the sun was already dipping on the horizon. "I need your help with something," I said desperately. "Tonight. As soon as the sun sets. It can't wait."

He opened the door for me. "What kind of help?"

"The magic mirror that shows me my night's work is stronger when both of us use it. My readings have been difficult since you lost your memory. Could you try tonight?"

He straightened slightly before answering. "Tell me what to do."

I placed the laptop bag on the kitchen counter and gestured toward the bedroom. He joined me as I pulled the stretch of silver that I used to see the future from his closet. I laid it on the wood floor between us.

"Sit across from me and rest your fingers on the edge, like this." I demonstrated our regular procedure, although usually we were naked. I didn't share that particular detail. He wasn't ready.

"What now?"

"Now, we open our connection and concentrate on where we need to patrol tonight."

I closed my eyes and focused, not on the mirror but on that gossamer thread that tethered us to each other. Our connection was strong, and I could read Rick's effort in the hum between us. But when I tried to draw on his power, to channel it into the mirror, all I got was a static throb in tempo with his heart. It wasn't that he was blocking me; I was in his head. The problem was, there was something missing. I could sense his trepidation, his desire to please me, but his power—the heart of what I used to draw on for this magic—was an empty pit. I blocked this thought from him, a hard task considering I was deep inside his head, and passed my hand over the mirror in front of me.

"Reveal." Power or no, the silver bubbled up before me. It stretched and morphed to form a quaint cobblestone street lined with historic buildings. "Looks like Salem," I said.

Rick remained silent, his eyes widening at the display between us.

"It's okay. This is supposed to happen," I said. The form of a human woman materialized in the alley. I memorized the landmarks as she walked the street, waiting for my target to appear, but the supernatural being I was supposed to capture and judge never came. Without warning, the woman collapsed dead in a pool of her own blood.

"What just happened?"

"The woman died," Rick offered.

"Did you see what attacked her?"

"Nothing attacked her. She just died," Rick said.

I looked over the mirror at him. Was Rick messing up my reading? It had never worked like this. I could always see the supernatural bad guy I was supposed to thwart. Was Rick's presence helping or hurting?

I forced a smile. "That's it. I've got my assignment. Thank you. You did great."

"Would you like me to come with you tonight?"

I chewed my lip. "Not yet. You need to learn to shift first or it could be dangerous."

He didn't say anything, but I could feel the bruise to his ego down our connection. "With how fast you're recovering, I'm sure it will be a matter of days before you get it."

In fact, Rick had attempted to shift without success almost every day since I'd rescued him from Tabetha, but nothing either I or my familiar, Poe, tried brought the beast to the surface. Rick's loss of memory seemed to run deep and include his magic. I was certain it was in there somewhere. I needed to find a way to draw it out.

"I'd better get to work," I said. I uncrossed my legs and began to rise from the floor, but Rick's hand shot out and grabbed my wrist.

"I'm sorry I'm not what you need me to be." His gaze met mine, and my heart melted.

I shook my head. "Rick, you are and always will be exactly what I need. Give it time. The evil witch who did this to you meant for it to be confusing. Tabetha didn't throw softballs. The spell she put on you was meant to break you. To break us. We just need to figure out how to put you back together."

He startled at my words and I instantly regretted my bluntness.

"And what if you can't 'put me back together'?" he asked, his tone as bitter as his glare.

I looked him in the eye and opened our connection as wide as it would go. If he had any thought-reading capability at all, he would sense what I was about to say was true. From the very heart of me, I promised, "If we can't get your memory back, then I'll take you just as you are.

CHAPTER 2
Familiarity

Power is a pain in the ass. People think they want it, they'll kill themselves to get it, but in the end, it's nothing but trouble. Take Tabetha's power; I was ringing with it. As I patrolled the street in Salem I'd seen in the mirror, the geraniums in the window boxes overhead stretched their necks in my direction. Don't get me started on the roses in my living room. I'd become the freaking Jolly Green Giant of witchdom. The summer night veritably buzzed around me as the elements of wind and wood tuned in to my presence.

So much power and so much responsibility. I hadn't asked for it, and I sure as hell didn't want it. But here I was.

"What exactly are we looking for?" Poe asked from my shoulder.

"Not sure. I couldn't tell from the mirror."

"What do you mean you couldn't tell? And, more importantly, why on earth are we here if you don't know what we are looking for?"

"There's an evil presence here. We saw a woman die. She fell twitching to the street. I couldn't see the perpetrator for some reason. Maybe she was poisoned, or it's some sort of poltergeist or invisible demon. All I know for sure is a supernatural being means to do a human harm, and it's our job to stop them." Again I wondered if the deficiency of vision was due to Rick's presence. I shook my head, not wanting it to be true. For all I knew, the enchanted mirror might be on the fritz.

"Mmm. It's *not* the mirror, and I doubt it's Rick," Poe said, doing that intuitive thing he did that made me feel like he was in my head. "If you ask me, without Rick's blood and, er, affections, your magic is weakening."

"Don't be ridiculous. I'm more powerful than ever. I can feel every blade of grass from here to Vermont."

"Yes, you have more power, but a more sizable engine requires a more sizable battery. You, Witcherella, are running on empty. The mirror knows and is answering in kind."

"Hmph." I hadn't considered this possibility, but Poe was probably right. It wasn't Rick's presence making the mirror go wonky; it was his absence. Three weeks had passed since I last enjoyed Rick's blood and as far as physical contact, that enjoyment ended at handholding. Every time I tried to get close to him, it was the fishing pole all over again. A distraction. An evasion. "I want Rick to come around on his terms. This is all new to him. He doesn't remember anything, especially not me. I was there, not so long ago, when I first met Rick and I didn't remember who *I* was. I need to be gentle with him."

"Sex can be gentle. Have I mentioned you're weakening?"

I groaned at his lack of subtlety. "It's not just about blood and sex," I murmured. "He either can't or won't shift or do magic of any kind. The answer is to jog his memory. I bought him a laptop today and showed him some cat videos."

"Cat videos?" Poe forced a gag.

I spread my hands. "I want him to learn about the modern world. LOL cats are the gateway drug. Oh, and that panda that sneezes. I love that one."

"Is he still hunting?"

"And fishing. Sometimes he stares blankly out the window," I said honestly. "Have you ever seen squirrel stew, Poe? It ain't pretty."

"Sounds delicious." Poe smacked his beak.

"I try to be charming, but it feels forced." I pressed a finger into my chin. "It is forced. We are two strangers, and I'm trying to force him to fall in love with me like a creeper. He probably wishes the entire thing was a bad dream. Plus, I think he might be depressed."

"Ya think? He falls asleep in 1698 and wakes up in 2015, having witnessed his fiancé burned at the stake and his entire community, including his parents, struck down by the cursed spellbook used to bind her. Of all the things Rick could be, depressed is the most logical."

"I don't know how to help him remember. I need him, Poe. If you're right about the mirror and my magic is waning, things are going to go downhill fast."

"Perhaps if you dressed a bit more comely?"

I looked down at my black T-shirt, jeans, and boots. My outfit was enchanted to remain comfortable in any weather and to bend and stretch to the demands of my job. I loved it. "What's wrong with this?"

"You have a skull and crossbones on your chest."

"It's fun. It says *dangerous, yet fashionably casual.*"

"It says *weird goth girl with emotional problems.*"

"You'd have emotional problems too if your fiancé left you at the altar and then forgot who you were. This is who I am." I stretched my arms to the sides. "Grateful Knight. Love me or leave me."

Poe cleared his throat. "Only problem is, if Rick doesn't love you and leaves you, it could mean your death. This is serious. If you can't bring back Rick's memories, at least try to make him want you. Tell him you need blood and sex, pronto. Love can happen at its own pace."

Love. I hoped it could happen at all. Sometimes Rick treated me like his captor, like he didn't quite trust me. I still loved him, even after he left me at the altar and ended up drugged in Tabetha's bed. Those are hard things to forgive, but I'd let them go. I loved Rick from a deep, forever place in my soul. A place that couldn't be reached by all the nastiness Tabetha had doled out before I tore her apart.

I rolled my eyes. Poe's concern for my well-being had as much to do with his existence being tied to mine as for my safety. I got it. I did. I couldn't go on much longer without Rick. But I also couldn't lose him. If I pushed him too hard, I might drive him away.

"What was that?" I said, perking my ears.

"What?"

"You didn't hear that? It was a twanging sound. Very faint. Like a guitar string being strung."

"Crap, Grateful. Move!" Poe took off from my shoulder, and I hit the pavement just in time. A silver arrow passed between us, where my head had been seconds ago. I leaped to my feet and drew Nightshade, searching the alley for the source of the shot. Platinum and black streaked behind an open window. I rushed toward the building, ducking inside the door.

Large blue eyes flashed from behind a six-foot stack of beer cases. A liquor store, although closed by the looks of things. A thick layer of dust covered the shelves and bottles.

"Come out and face your judgment." Nightshade's blue glow filled the room. "I'll be merciful if you make this easy."

A metallic laugh echoed through the store, bouncing off the glass bottles around me. My face tightened. Only one person laughed like that. Soleil. It was a fae laugh. I cursed under my breath. Fecking fae. The creatures were infinitely diverse and harder than hell to kill.

The twang of his bow rang through the room, and I shifted, putting a shelf of bourbon between us. The effort was futile. The arrow sliced through the metal shelf like butter and shattered a bottle of Jack Daniels beside my ducking head. Whatever kind of fae this was, he was playing for keeps.

I went possum, flopping to the floor and rolling to my back. With a painful moan, I grabbed the fallen arrow. Silver shaft and tip. Hawk feather fletching branded with a circular symbol. Wait. I'd seen this symbol before somewhere.

Nightshade hummed to me in warning. I tucked the arrow under my neck and closed my eyes to the narrowest of slits. I didn't hear him coming until he was standing over me. Definitely fae.

It was hard to concentrate on anything beyond the arrow pointed at my head, but I forced myself as he drew near. Platinum silver hair fell blade straight from a widow's peak, framing a pale complexion that housed oversized blue eyes and full red lips. Despite the white hair, his skin was taut and wrinkle free, and he carried the vibrancy of youth. He wore a black suit with the same familiar circular symbol bronzed and pinned to his lapel. Some fae, like sprites and pixies, were smaller in stature, but he was human-sized, at least six foot, with a lanky but muscular build. I could never mistake him for human though because he approached me fluidly, like his feet never touched the floor, his bones and joints flexible things, lithe and supple. He lowered the point of his arrow toward my nose.

With superhuman speed, I sprang up and rotated sideways, the night air lifting me. Nightshade circled, slicing through the drawn arrow. The silver arrowhead rattled to the floor. My target didn't hesitate for a moment. The bottom of his bow flipped up, catching me under the chin and knocking my head back. Through swirling stars, I saw him draw another arrow, lightning fast, and take a step back to aim.

I pushed through the lights dancing in my vision, ducked under his releasing arrow, and tackled him into the bourbon. The shelf toppled, liquor and glass spraying around our crashing bodies. I scrambled to get the upper hand, but I hadn't counted on the bottles. Broken glass shredded me. Blood rushed in crimson rivulets down the outside of my arms and from a particularly large gash in my leg. The more I struggled, the more I bled. With one hand braced on a metal shelf near my ear, I fought to get my feet under me, wedging them between two of the lower projections. The fae's gloved fist pounded into my ribcage, knocking me back into the glass and metal.

His opposite fist hammered toward my throat. I blocked, grunting as my forearm took the force of it. I jammed my foot between us and kicked as I called on the wind to lift me out of the rubble. My magic answered me but weakly. Just enough to get me out of the mess, but not enough to get away. A fizzle instead of a boom. I scrambled to the front of the store, angling between the stack of beer cases and a big picture window.

"Give yourself up. You're going to the hellmouth," I called.

There was a slap and the beer toppled. I dodged the heavy cases, the glass and suds spraying from the impact with the floor. The fae rushed me, his face in mine in no time. I had the advantage. His bow was gone, thrown from us in the scuffle. Nightshade, on the other hand, was still in my grip. I kicked as hard as I could into his stomach to put space between us.

He yelped in pain and bared his teeth. Stepping back, I placed Nightshade's glowing tip to his neck. "I sentence you—"

Usually, the glow would wrap around my target and transport them to the hellmouth at my condemnation, but my judgment stuck in my throat as Nightshade petered out, and her blade became normal bone. "What the hellmouth?" I cursed.

A punch landed in my side, folding me in half. Nightshade didn't fail me this time. Enchanted or not, she sliced, skimming my side and severing the wrist of my attacker. Silver blood sprayed as the fae recoiled, a tinny scraped-metal shriek breaking his full red lips. I backed away, shaking Nightshade to try to get her to work. How was I supposed to send this baddie on if she wouldn't enforce my judgment?

The fae lowered his shoulder and barreled into me. My feet left the floor, and we crashed through the picture window, glass shredding what was left of my exposed skin. The force of the impact threw Nightshade from my grip, and I landed in the street, covered in silver fae blood courtesy of his spurting wrist.

"Ow! What the f—?" Where the silver blood hit my wounds, my skin sizzled and foamed like acid. I screamed and thrashed, trying to brush the stuff off me. It stuck like tar.

"Stupid witch." The creature crawled off me and cuddled his bloody stump to his chest. "Goblin blood is poisonous to your kind. You're as good as dead."

Goblin? I knew almost nothing about goblins. Less than nothing. That they existed was the extent of my education. At the moment, I sorely regretted my lack of edification.

My muscles twitched and hardened. Rigid, shivering, I couldn't swallow. Foam filled my mouth and spilled over the side of my face. I gagged and coughed reflexively. The cobblestone street was cold and uncomfortable under my head and back.

"You did it, Tobias!" A female goblin came into view beside the one called Tobias. The two were almost identical, blue eyes twinkling as if my impending death was a huge victory. She tucked her long white hair behind a pointy ear, exposing a bronze symbol pinned to her lapel. It was the same symbol as on the arrow fletching, and it seemed to taunt me with its vague familiarity. "This is a proud day. There will be much celebration."

"I need the doctor," Tobias moaned, hugging his bleeding stump.

In cold blood, the female drew her bow and released an arrow into my shoulder, unnecessary considering I was dying anyway. *Bitch.* My muscles rigid, I couldn't even flinch from the pain.

"Come, brother." She stepped over my body to wrap her arm around his shoulders and help him away to whatever doctor treated silver-blooded goblins.

They left me there to die. *I* was the woman I'd seen dying in the street! My breath gurgled in my bloody throat. The pain was excruciating as the neurotoxin worked its way to my lungs. I could barely draw air as it was, but as the venom did its dirty work, my inhales whistled as if my throat was closing off. I tried to reach out with my magic, but I was too weak. I couldn't even sense Nightshade in my current condition.

My eyes burned. I'd lost my ability to blink. All the muscles of my face had frozen in place. I took one last tight breath and thought of Rick. If I did die and was reincarnated now, there would be no one to help him get his memories back. No one to help the new me find her magic. No one to manage the Monk's Hill or Salem wards in my absence.

I tried to release the breath I was holding but couldn't, and I couldn't draw another one. Spots danced in my vision, and then, despite my eyelids being locked open, the world around me turned black as night, and I slipped into oblivion.

CHAPTER 3
Dangerous Liaisons

As a reincarnated witch, you would think I'd be used to dying, but apparently death never loses its edge. My lungs ached, the neurotoxin rendering them unable to release the air trapped inside me. I was frozen, vulnerable, and slowly succumbing to the creeping darkness of death. I silently said goodbye to Rick, to my father, Michelle, Poe... where was Poe, anyway?

Warm liquid washed over my arms and legs, my face, my open eyes, into my mouth. The shock of the dousing revived me, and I tried again to breathe.

"Come on, Hecate. Don't disappoint me by feigning ineptitude." Julius's smooth voice slipped through my mind—the leader of the free vampire coven in Carlton City and unexpected ally as of late.

I swallowed the pool of liquid on my tongue and sputtered as my throat obeyed. A magic potion? Julius had found a secret magical antidote for goblin poison. And it tasted good! Like... like... "Wine?" I rasped.

"I thought the fermented Pinot might have a neutralizing effect on goblin venom. The creature's magic comes from the metal element. Its blood is effectively smothering the wind and wood in yours. Grapes are a product of wood and earth. Fermentation introduces gases to the mix. As such, it should have healing properties for you." There was a pause, the sound of a cork popping from a bottle, and then more splashing against my skin. "Perhaps your affinity for the beverage has kept you alive tonight. Regardless, you are one lucky witch that I happened to be near when your familiar came for me. You are at death's door. I'd venture to say a minute from the grave."

My eyes began to work again, and I blinked them against a sea of deep red. I was back inside the liquor store. I couldn't move my limbs, but I could see Julius. Dressed in a blue silk shirt and trousers smudged with my blood, he hovered above me, an open bottle of wine in one hand and what looked like scotch in the other. His chocolate waves curled perfectly behind his ears. As usual, he looked almost human, aside from his too-large navy-blue eyes. Vampires had some illusive abilities, but under it all they were nocturnal creatures.

"What's the scotch for?" I croaked.

He took a deep swig from the bottle in his opposite hand, then raised it as if to toast me. "The scotch is for steadying my nerves. Goblins are nothing to mess with, Grateful. You should know better."

As if I'd done it on purpose. "Help me," I sputtered.

He dumped more wine over my shivering limbs. "What do you think I'm doing? Although, I am sorry I can't do more. I've neutralized the poison, but I fear the damage is done. Your internal organs are a bit overcooked even for the magic of Pinot Noir." He tossed the bottle over his shoulder where it shattered against the fallen shelf, then retrieved another bottle from a display and popped the cork.

"Poe?"

"Your familiar flew in the direction of home. I presume to retrieve your caretaker, although we both know he won't be coming."

"He's fine." I groaned in pain.

Julius knelt by my side, his superhuman speed making it appear as if he zapped in and out of existence. "Do you know why I was close enough to help you? I've been following you for weeks, Grateful. He hasn't patrolled once since his run-in with Tabetha. Can he shift? Does he even remember how to drive a car?"

"You've been following me?" I closed my eyes, too weak to argue. He was right. Rick probably wouldn't come, and I was hurt—bad. I could feel myself slipping under again, like I was drowning. My breath rattled and, as a nurse, I was well aware rattling was a bad sign.

"Following you, yes. I find myself drawn to you, in fact," Julius said softly. "Despite myself. It's an unnatural thing for a vampire to take an interest in a witch, and I am an old vampire who has seen many unnatural things."

"I need Rick," I whimpered.

"You are bleeding," Julius murmured in a breathy, lover's voice. His lips were close. The glass had shredded most of my exposed skin, and I could feel warm blood drip down my face, over my chin, and across my neck to pool in the recess between my clavicles. He fixated on that heavy, wet spot.

"Don't do it, Julius. You won't be able to stop. You'll kill me. I can't lose any more blood."

Long, tapered fingers ran through my wine-and-blood-soaked hair. Gently. Lovingly. He lowered his face until his nose almost touched mine. "I would never hurt you, Grateful. Don't you see how we've helped each other these past weeks? We are friends now, yes? Maybe more."

In fact, Julius's help had been a godsend in Rick's absence. It wasn't the first time he'd shown up when I needed him, although this time he was a little late to the party. He'd sworn to be my ally and had kept his side of the bargain. Still, I didn't like the way he stared at my jugular.

His lips lowered to the base of my neck. The slurping made me cringe as he drank the pool of blood there, then licked along my shoulder to my ear. His tongue gripped like sandpaper, like a cat's. I grimaced.

"Please don't," I whispered, bracing myself for the bite.

Although his fangs grazed my skin, and I could hear him swallow, he did not strike. I opened my eyes to find his nose almost touching mine again, his eyes wide, pupils dilated, my blood on his lips.

"You are very near death," he said.

"I need Rick." My throat was dry and raw.

"There is another way."

His nocturnal blue eyes twinkled. He raised his right wrist to his mouth and bit. "Drink my blood. It will heal you."

I shook my head. "I don't want to be a vampire."

"A witch cannot become a vampire, but I have read of witches drawing on a vampire's eternal life. If the legends are true, my blood will temporarily give you qualities of a vampire. It will heal you and make you harder to kill. All you have to do is drink."

A bubble of thick blood formed on his wrist. My head was foggy, and the room wavered like a boat at sea. I didn't completely trust Julius, but I was dying. What would happen to Rick and our territory if I did? Did I have a choice but to try Julius's way?

I parted my lips. His blood was thicker than human blood, and the first drop came concentrated and syrupy. I closed my eyes and waited for it to hit my tongue.

"Don't drink that," Polina's voice said. I opened my eyes to see my half-sister, the redheaded witch from Smuggler's Notch. I hadn't seen her since the night we rescued her from her underground prison, buried under Tabetha's magical landscaping. She'd helped me kill the evil wood witch and had earned my trust. Now, her hand hovered between my mouth and Julius's wrist. His fangs were out, and a deep growl rumbled from his chest.

"Grateful, tell your vampire to back off," Polina said.

"Julius, please. Leave her alone."

The vampire retreated from us in a graceful bending of crouched limbs. Polina wiped his blood on my wine-soaked jeans. "Thank the goddess I made it here on time. And thank your familiar. He risked his life for you."

Poe landed on my other side and laid his head on my chest. He looked like I felt. Large patches of feathers had molted from his back and wings. As my familiar, if I was dying, he was dying too.

"Don't you remember my warning about letting a vampire drink your blood?" Polina admonished.

"Vaguely."

"Julius has had your blood three times. He's bound himself to you."

"What's that mean?"

"It means he is yours to control as you please."

I scrunched my brow slightly, a movement that made my face hurt. "Why would he do that?"

"Judging by this"—she held up her bloody palm—"it appears he was planning for you to bind yourself to him too."

"He said it would heal me."

Polina frowned. "It would. Unfortunately, it would also make you his as he is yours. You'd be metaphysically bound. I don't think you want that, do you?"

I shot an accusing look at Julius. "No."

Julius inhaled sharply as if we'd insulted him. "I did no such thing. I am not bound to the witch, nor trying to bind her. Only to save her."

"Ignorance of magical law does not negate magical law." Polina shrugged. "You drank her blood three times. That binds you. If she drinks your blood, she is bound to you." She turned back to me and whispered. "I think you've broken his heart."

Julius grunted, looking disgusted. "Is this true?" he asked me.

"You're asking the wrong witch," I mumbled.

"Can it be undone?" Julius demanded.

Polina's lips pursed with disapproval. "What is done cannot be undone. The bond must run its course."

"How long will that take?" Julius demanded.

With a roll of her eyes, Polina responded, "Likely the length of her natural life."

Julius scowled.

"I need Rick," I said to both of them. "Or he won't be bound to me for long."

She flipped her long red braid behind her back. "I'm here to help. Poe was smart to send Hildegard to find me, although I fear your raven is in as dire straits as you." She gently pressed the flesh around the arrow protruding from my shoulder, and I moaned in pain.

"Don't pull it out. I'll bleed to death if you do," I said, drawing on my experience as an ER nurse.

"Agreed. I apologize in advance. I'm going to get you to Rick fast, but this may hurt a little. The way a metal witch travels isn't as glamorous as some, but I'll get you where you need to go."

"How does a metal witch travel?"

Polina gathered me into her lap and reached into the heavy bag at her hip. "Take her blade and meet us at Rick's cottage," she said to Julius.

He didn't move.

"Tell him," she said to me.

"Why can't I take it with me?" I asked her.

"Your blade is made of bone, and you alone can wield it. But as your servant, Julius can transport it for you. I can't."

Through cracked lips, I said, "Julius, please take my blade to Rick's." In a flash, he was gone and so was Nightshade.

Polina pulled a fistful of glittering gold dust from her leather satchel and held it over our heads. Poe's heart pounded ominously against mine, and I tried to comfort him by cradling his body to my chest.

"What is that?" I asked.

"Gold dust."

I narrowed my eyes at her. "How does a metal witch travel, Polina?"

She sighed. "By metal." She opened her fist.

Instinctively, I took a deep breath and held it. It was an excellent strategy. We came apart in a swirl of metallic pieces, and I found out the hard way exactly how a metal witch travels.

CHAPTER 4
The Guilt Trip

I learned something traveling with Polina. There's metal everywhere, mostly in the form of pipes. We washed through the waterworks, squeezed through rocks lined with veins of iron, and even followed a few electrical wires. Our travels ended with my entire body pouring out of Rick's kitchen faucet. I rolled off the edge of the sink and landed painfully on his linoleum.

"Ouch," I said. I'd dropped Poe in transit, and he landed by my side looking as disheveled as I felt. A cloud of mangy black feathers he couldn't afford to lose shed to the floor as he shivered next to me, conspicuously quiet.

Polina was the last through the spigot but unlike our painful arrival, she leaped from the faucet and landed on her toes, oddly invigorated. Her braid had come undone in our travels, and her hair floated around her in wild red waves that only enhanced her otherworldly quality.

"Woot! That was one hell of a ride, wasn't it?" she said, circling her arm above her head.

I groaned.

"Sorry, Grateful. Traveling by gold dust is a lot to get used to, especially for an injured air and wood witch. To say I took you out of your element would be an understatement. I'm just happy I got you here in one piece. I mean, they say metal chops wood. I might have sliced and diced you if I wasn't careful. But here we are, and you're still breathing—"

"Polina?" I cut her off. She rambled when she was nervous, and I could tell she'd had major anxiety about my potential survival.

"Yes?"

"Get Rick."

She moved to leave the kitchen, but there was no need. Rick was standing at the threshold, staring at me with wide, terrified eyes. As always was the case lately, Rick's vulnerable expression did not match his overtly masculine appearance. His size, as well as his dark waves and Mediterranean complexion, gave him a forceful presence that seemed to fill the space between us.

"Oh, good." Polina pointed at me. "You've got to give her your blood. Now. She's dying."

Rick stared at me, the corner of his mouth twisting downward as if the mere thought turned his stomach. "She is gravely injured," he said.

"Thank you, Mr. Obvious. Did you hear me?" Polina said. "She will die if you don't feed her your blood, right now."

Wood slammed against stone as the front door was thrown open, and Julius rushed to my side. He pushed Rick into the wall in his effort to get to me. Only vampire strength could explain the way Rick's feet left the floor, and his body dented the drywall from Julius's efforts. My caretaker brushed himself off, looking rightfully peeved.

"I can help her," Julius said. "Drink of me." He lifted his wrist to his fangs.

"Hold it right there, cowboy!" Polina said, grabbing Julius's wrist. She turned her attention to Rick, who'd become statuesque in the threshold to the tiny kitchen. "Are you going to let him do this? You're her caretaker!"

Rick seemed paralyzed by the situation. He'd had my blood plenty of times, but never given me his. I'd never pressed the issue. I assumed he wasn't ready to take that step. As his mouth opened and closed with unsaid words, I could see my mistake. Now he had the trauma of me near death and was being guilted and pressured by people he didn't even know.

"Don't force him," I croaked. All I wanted was to close my eyes. I was fading fast.

Julius stroked my cheek. "Let me help you." The vampire leaned over me, smelling of scotch and the forest at night. I blinked at him, unable to respond.

A hand landed on Julius's shoulder and yanked, the vampire's head snapping with the force of his retreat.

Rick's hand twisted into the vampire's silk collar, holding him away from me.

"Tell me what to do," Rick said, shoving Julius across the kitchen.

"Score your wrist with your teeth," Polina instructed. She raised her arm to her mouth to demonstrate.

Rick followed suit, but when he bit, he hardly broke the skin.

"You've got to shift partially," Polina said. "Your human teeth will barely draw a drop, and your flesh won't heal as quickly if you don't."

With a shake of his head, Rick admitted, "I can't shift."

Julius grabbed the sides of his head, clawing at his hair and turning a pleading gaze toward me. "This, this derelict is why you won't drink my blood? A caretaker who can't shift?"

Black spots danced in my vision. I was slipping away again. "Carry me to the bed," I whispered. "I don't want to die on the floor." I closed my eyes.

A deep feral growl rumbled through the kitchen, and strong arms swept me up. My head rolled against a broad chest. Next to my ear, the steady beat of a heart comforted me. I didn't have to open my eyes to know it was Rick who held me. He was gentle, positioning me to avoid the arrow still protruding from my shoulder, and trying his best not to jostle me too much.

Carefully, he sat down in his bed with me cradled in his arms. My eyelids fluttered. Through our connection, I felt his worry for me. He wrapped an arm around my head and offered his wrist. "Perhaps if you did it?"

"Too weak." I couldn't if I tried. I was too exhausted and in debilitating pain. "Nightshade," I blurted. "My blade is enchanted."

"Where is it?" he asked.

I whispered, "Julius." The vampire appeared in the bedroom door in an instant.

"Bring her blade," Rick commanded.

The vampire didn't move. "Julius, please," I said weakly. The request was barely audible, but Julius retrieved the blade and offered me the hilt.

I searched Rick's face. "You'll have to do it."

This made Julius's lips peel back from his fangs in disgust. "*I* could draw blood from the caretaker if needed."

With a growl, Rick wrapped his hand around the hilt and drew the blade quickly across his wrist. He lowered the bleeding cut to my mouth. Warm ambrosia coursed down my throat, hit my stomach, and radiated to my fingers and toes. I moaned and closed my eyes at the taste, the nourishment I'd been denied for so long.

"Out of the way, vampire," Polina said. Her small fingers brushed my shoulder as she gripped the arrow. "On the count of three. One… two… three." I swallowed a scream around Rick's wrist as the arrow tore from my flesh. My eyes popped open, and I lost my grip on his arm.

When I caught my breath, he repositioned me in his lap. "Leave us," he told the others.

"Please. Please help me," I begged, searching his face. The small amount of blood I'd had was counteracting the venom, but the process felt like I was on fire. I didn't notice the witch or the vampire leave until the door clicked shut. I'm usually not a crier, but tears of pain drenched my cheeks.

"Come. Drink more," Rick whispered, slicing a fresh gash in his wrist and plugging my mouth with it. I sucked greedily, the pain withdrawing with every swallow. Slowly, the cuts on my arms began to heal. He repositioned my back against his chest and stroked the hair from my face.

"Grateful," he whispered in my ear. "It is working." His breath was warm and soft.

With a long inhale through my nose, I settled into his lap, falling into a rhythm of deep draws and audible swallows. I reached behind me for his other arm and wrapped it around my torso, resting his palm between my breasts and pressing my back into his chest.

His broken exhale was my reward. He felt it too, the rush of heat that came when we shared blood. I was full, in fact, moderately sloshy from all the blood, but didn't want to move. This was the closest we'd been physically in weeks. I stopped drinking but licked the cut on his wrist with long, languid strokes of my tongue.

He didn't protest or push me away. On the contrary, the hard length of him twitched under me. I stopped licking and adjusted myself in his lap to look at him. What I saw made my heart leap. His eyes were black and his jaw slightly elongated. He pulled his upper body away from me, pressing into the headboard.

"It's okay," I said. "It's just your beast coming to the surface. Your beast likes to get in on the action." I smiled and cupped the side of his face, stroking the line of his jaw.

He pulled away, shaking his head violently until he appeared fully human again. "I don't want to hurt you. I don't... think I can control it. My body..." He rubbed a hand down his T-shirt.

"Your body is doing what it was made to do. You want me," I whispered. "You want to be with me. It's perfectly natural for your body to change like that. It knows what it wants." I placed my hands on his chest and repositioned myself to straddle his lap. Inhaling his scent, I lowered my lips to within an inch of his.

His startled expression stopped me before I made contact. "Is this... intimacy normal in this time?" He bit his lip and allowed his gaze to rake down my body. "I wouldn't dream of touching you like this in mine. It would ruin your reputation and my virtue." He swallowed, his lips parting as he focused on mine with barely contained desire.

"Totally normal now," I lied. "People do it all the time." Not so much of a lie. I rolled my hips, grinding against him, and glory hallelujah if he didn't respond in kind. "It's okay for us because we were married," I murmured. "It's like I told you. We've been together for hundreds of years. We're supposed to be together." The tips of my nipples brushed his chest. Too much? Was I pushing him too far too fast?

If I considered slowing down, that thought dissolved in the sound of his moan.

I pressed my lips against his.

His breath hitched in his throat, and he pulled back slightly. "I hardly know you."

"Then get to know me." I pressed my lips into his again, breathing deeply through my nose and using my arms around his neck to pull him closer. Still, he held himself in check. His kiss was guarded and distant. I rolled my hips, begging him with my body to respond.

Until an invisible barrier between us shattered. He stroked along my sides and up my back, pressing his lips into mine. He parted his mouth and allowed my tongue to trail over his lower lip. There was a moment of hesitation and then he responded, stroking with his tongue. I groaned with desire.

His hands explored my body, wild and inexperienced. I didn't mind as long as he kept touching me. Energy swirled thick around us, leeching into my skin, bolstering my soul.

"Isabella," he murmured.

I tried to ignore it. I should have let it go. Did it really matter that he called me by the name of a woman I used to be? Yes. Yes, it did. I pulled back. "Grateful," I corrected.

He visibly cooled, the last remnants of the beast bleeding away. Confusion tightened his brow.

"You're not ready." I shook my head, heart pounding. I was still in his lap, but the distance between us might've put me in the next room. I could've cried for want of him.

A knock on the door broke the awkward tension.

"Julius, have a seat. I'll be out when I'm good and ready," I yelled.

"I apologize for the interruption," Polina called through the door. "Julius has gone. The sun is rising, and he needed to return to his tomb. I would show myself out, but I must speak with you before I go."

Curious about the urgency in Polina's voice, I asked, "About what?'"

"About why the goblin who tried to kill you had a symbol of our sisterhood on his arrow."

CHAPTER 5
A Theory

I removed myself from the comfort of Rick's arms reluctantly, scooting off his lap and onto my feet. As soon as I was off him, he pitched forward, resting his elbows on his knees and digging his hands into his hair. A mix of relief and disappointment poured down our connection. I hated interrupting what was a major breakthrough for us. We had attraction, albeit misaligned with my previous incarnation, Isabella. I was sure with a little time and focus I could turn that into something more—something directed at me. Rick had shifted, a little. That meant his magic was there, under the surface. He just didn't remember how to use it.

But for both of our sakes, I needed to know more about the goblin who'd tried to kill me in Salem. "I'll be right back," I told Rick.

He took a deep breath and nodded toward the door.

I slipped out of the room and joined Polina near the sofa. "Are you familiar with the symbol on the fletching?" I asked her.

My redheaded half-sister held up the arrow that almost killed me, the symbol branded into the fletching taunting me with its familiarity. "This is our mother's symbol. Hecate's wheel."

"That's where I've seen it before. When Hecate gave me permission to kill Tabetha, it was on the door to her jungle abode." I lifted the arrow from her fingers, inspecting it from all angles. I called for my familiar, anxious to learn what he knew about it. "Poe!"

"He's gone," Polina said, taking the arrow back from me. "Once he was feeling better, I let him and Hildie out to go hunting. Said he was starving."

I rubbed my stomach. "I know the feeling. Can I talk you into a snack? Maybe a hot beverage?"

"I'd like that. Thank you."

In the kitchen, I found some tea and a tin of butter cookies from Christmas at the back of the cupboard. I popped the tin open, relieved the cookies weren't stale, then filled the teakettle. Once I lit the stove under the teapot, I got down to the matter at hand.

"The symbol seemed familiar to me, but I couldn't remember where I'd seen it," I said.

"You'll find it at the back of your spellbook and every Hecate grimoire. The circular symbol represents her labyrinth, her duties as the goddess of the crossroads, death, doorways, or change." She traced the circular symbol. "There are three areas where the maze bubbles out. They represent her three aspects—maiden, mother, and crone. The star at the center is a depiction of the united elements, the source of her power."

I shook my head. "Why is Hecate's symbol on a goblin arrow?"

"Or more to the point, why does the Goblin Trinate want you dead?"

"Goblin Trinate?"

"All goblins are dangerous, but the one that shot you was the most dangerous type of all. Similar to the fae, there are many varieties of goblins. From an evolutionary standpoint, they are presumed to be cousins of the fae, actually. But only one type of goblin uses a bow and arrow like this. These goblins are organized and humanoid. You might think of them as the goblin equivalent of the mafia. They call themselves the Goblin Trinate, and—this is the important part, Grateful—they have a reputation as mercenaries."

"You think someone hired them to kill me?"

"I don't know. I'm simply saying it's possible. The more likely scenario is you caught the goblin in the act of doing something else, and he felt threatened by your judgment."

I tapped my fingers near the arrow, trying to digest everything she'd said. I'd gone to Salem to judge and sentence a maleficent supernatural being. That being had turned on me. That wasn't surprising. It happened almost every time I patrolled my ward. But this encounter was different.

"My power faded when I tried to sentence him to the hellmouth. Nightshade just fizzled."

Polina looked at me out the corner of her eye. "Was your blade touching goblin blood? The blood has anti-magical properties, which is why it's poisonous to witches."

"I don't think so, but there was so much glass and spilled liquor. Maybe."

"There had to be blood. Hecates like us have power over all supernatural beings."

I tried to remember for sure, but I couldn't. "There was something else. The goblin's name was Tobias. I know this because his sister showed up as I was dying in the street. She congratulated him on killing me and said there would be much celebration among their kind."

This time Polina grabbed a cookie from the tin. "That sounds premeditated," she said nervously before stuffing it into her mouth.

"My thoughts exactly." I rolled the base of the fletching between my fingers, the feathers revolving between us. "Maybe this is a clue. What does the symbol mean, anyway? Have they always used it? Or is this a calling card from the one who hired them? Is the symbol about me—an arrow with my name on it, so to speak?" I popped a cookie in my mouth and then another, hoping the sugar and fat would numb the anxiety snowballing within me.

"I'm not sure. Trinate means 'group of three,' so the symbol is apropos for their organization. It could be a coincidence, or maybe it's a form of goddess worship. I actually wish Fang Face had stayed. Julius has been around long enough to know for sure. I'm at a loss. My ward is rural. We have massive troll problems but no goblins."

"If they weren't working for someone else, why might the Goblin Trinate want me dead?"

Polina leaned against the counter, toying with the ends of her wild red hair. "I'm not sure, but no scenario I can think of bodes well for you."

"That's comforting." The teapot whistled. I turned the burner off and added the tea bags. "Just for kicks and giggles, what scenarios can you think of?"

"Scenario one is that the goblins are making a power play for control of your new ward. With Tabetha so recently dead, they probably thought you were an easy target. No witch means no judgment."

I nod. "Very possible. If it's true, it's a good thing they believe I'm dead. What else?"

She spread her hands and shrugged. "Before you killed Tabetha, Hecate gave you permission to kill her, right?"

"Uh-huh."

"Well, you probably weren't the only one. If word was out that Salem's witch was on Hecate's hit list, maybe you were a case of mistaken identity."

"They mistook me for Tabetha because I am now the witch of Salem."

"Right."

"Wouldn't they know what she looked like?"

"Not necessarily. I've never seen a goblin in person. I can't imagine they kept close company with Tabetha."

I dug two mugs out of the cupboard and poured us both a cup of tea. "So… what's scenario three?"

She brought the mug to her lips and took a long sip. "I think we should consider the possibility that Mother wants you dead."

I swallowed down the wrong pipe and burst into a fit of coughing. When I'd finally managed to cough up the wayward tea, I asked, "Why?" But I knew why. I wasn't supposed to accept Tabetha's grimoire. I wasn't supposed to have power over two elements.

"You know why. It's because you took Tabetha's grimoire," Polina confirmed. "The question is why she would be so indirect about it. Why doesn't she just smite you from the earth?"

Without any explanation for not being smote, I had no choice but to shove three more cookies into my mouth and shrug.

Polina sighed. "If she wanted you dead, you'd be dead. Which means that particular scenario probably is not true."

I'd raised my mug to wash down the cookies when Rick appeared beside Polina. He lifted the arrow between his fingers, staring at the symbol.

"Do you recognize that, Rick?"

"No," he said. "But it seems familiar to me, like I used to, a long time ago."

"I had the same reaction."

"It is said that her symbol is stamped upon the hearts of her progeny," Polina said.

Rick returned the arrow to the counter. "You are lucky to be alive."

I furrowed my brow, curious about something. "Polina, you said that Poe found Hildegard and Hildegard found you and that's how you knew to help me, but Poe couldn't have made it to Vermont in his condition. How did it happen?"

She sighed. "I was already on my way to you, although I had no idea it was you. I saw your death in my mirror."

"You have one too?" I raised my eyebrows.

"Who do you think made yours?"

"Rick told me I conjured it in a past life."

Polina chuckled, holding her stomach. "Conjured it from where? Only a metal witch could make such a thing. I told you we were friends before. It was a gift."

"And you have one too?"

"I have several. A smaller one I keep with me at all times and a more powerful one at my home, too big to move. It works the same way."

I scratched behind my ear, the dried blood in my hair flaking under my fingertips. I desperately needed a shower. "Polina…" I said, distracted by the way the light broke through the window and illuminated Rick's muscled physique. I was still hungry, and today had been a breakthrough. I turned back to her so I could concentrate. "Did you see the goblin in your mirror? Is that why you came?"

"Yes. I'm sorry I didn't recognize it was you. Your human status confused me."

Crap. I was right about the mirror. Something was off with Rick and me beyond his memory. It might've been my need for blood, but I had a sinking feeling in my gut it could be more.

Polina rubbed her hands together. "You know, Grateful, there's only one way to find out for sure why the goblins tried to kill you today."

I squinted one eye and scowled. "You're not suggesting…"

"We go over and confront Mother. Not directly, of course." Polina coiled her hair around one finger.

"We can't ask her. Mother hates questions."

"No. We don't ask. We tell. And we see how she responds. I'll go with you for support. If both of us are there, we can play it off as concern over a possible goblin coup rather than her presumed murderous tendencies."

I crinkled my nose. "I don't like this. Facing the goddess was not on my to-do list today."

Polina laughed so hard she snorted. "Mine either. In fact, I've got to get home and check on my ward. Tonight? At midnight? We can go over from your attic."

I nodded. "I can't thank you enough. For everything."

"I owe you." She winked. "See you tonight."

I gave her a quick hug. She reached into her bag for a pinch of gold dust and sprinkled it over her head. Her body twisted and disappeared into the faucet.

"Her method of travel disturbs me," Rick said from beside me. He frowned at the kitchen sink and crossed his arms over his chest.

"I'm not crazy about it either." I fidgeted as an awkward silence descended between us. "Thank you for your blood. You saved my life."

"What sort of man would I be if I did not help a woman in distress? I don't remember you, or this time, but I know who I am."

Okay. That didn't bolster my hope of continuing where we left off. It sounded like he would have done it for anyone, not just me. I bit my lip, disappointed I'd misread his signals. "Rick, about what happened earlier…" He blushed crimson and I changed my angle. "Would you like to go on a real date?" I blew out a deep breath. "You don't remember me but, maybe, you could get to know me."

The corner of Rick's mouth lifted and the twinkle returned to his gray eyes. "I would enjoy that, ever much, Grateful."

"Still Grateful, huh?"

"What else would I call you?"

"Before, you used to call me, *mi cielo*."

"My sky." He laughed. "My grandmother used to call me that. I must have loved you very much."

I glanced down at the floor. "You did. Just as I loved you." My voice came out hardly a whisper. I'd shared stories with Rick before, tried to explain how things were between us, but this was the most receptive he'd ever been.

His shadow passed over me, and I looked up to find him close enough to touch. His Adam's apple bobbed with a hard swallow as he searched my face. "It's been overwhelming."

"I understand."

He licked his lips. "But I haven't been fair to you. You need more of me than you've let on before today."

"I didn't want to pressure you."

"I am not a man to shirk my responsibilities."

"I want to be more to you than a responsibility," I said under my breath.

He rested his hands on my shoulders, sending a wave of anticipatory heat through me. My body hungered for him. Rick inhaled slowly, nostrils flaring. He felt it too. This thing between us was alive and utterly undeniable. His mind may not know me, but his body did.

"I want to try. I want to learn who you are. If I am what you say I am, I want to work to get my memories back. I want to be what you need me to be."

"How could you not be?" I asked, cupping his face. The draw between us was powerful, like two magnets only held apart by force of will. I leaned in, intending to kiss him and was surprised when he pushed me away.

"Grateful, let's do this the right way. We've been through too much to ruin something that hasn't had a chance to start."

I cleared my throat and forced myself to take a step back. "I, er, sure." I looked at my watch awkwardly. "F—" I halted my curse at the look on Rick's face. In 1698, proper women did not curse like sailors. "I'm late for work."

Rushing from the kitchen, I gathered Nightshade from the bedroom. I was about to exit through the front door when he called to me.

"When is our date?" Rick asked.

I smiled. "Tomorrow. Noon. I'll take you on a picnic." I left, remembering my first date with Rick, a picnic on Monk's Hill that had ended in lovemaking. I hoped tomorrow would end in precisely the same way.

CHAPTER 6
Wine O'Clock

Twelve hours later, I shouldered my front door open, finished working the hospital shift from hell. I didn't close the door behind me. The stench in my house was stifling, and I needed the fresh air. My entire place reeked of roses, Tabetha's roses. The witch was exacting her revenge by way of a vine of red blooms eternally coiling around my banister. I'd succeeded in containing the roses to the stairwell, but no matter what spells I tried from either of my magical grimoires, I could not keep the flowers from growing or blooming.

I tossed my keys toward the kitchen island from the foyer. They didn't make it. With a clang, they hit the wood floor. No way was I bending down to pick them up. I hit the couch. Face first. In my scrubs. And started blubbering like a kid who dropped their ice cream cone.

With my head buried in a floral pillow, I heard rather than saw Poe fly down the stairwell and land on the sofa arm.

"Who died?" he asked sarcastically.

Asshole. I looked at him out of the corner of my eye. "My father."

Poe gasped in disbelief. "What happened?"

"Nothing. Dad is fine. But it serves you right for being so sarcastic about my emotional breakdown. What if it *was* serious?"

"But it's not, is it?" He rolled his black eyes. "That was not funny! I've grown quite fond of your dear old dad. We live in dangerous times. You shouldn't joke about such things."

"Bite me." I buried my face in the pillow again.

"What has your undies in a bunch?"

I sat up and rested my feet on the coffee table. "Not only do I have to face my mother tonight, a woman who happens to be a vengeful goddess responsible for at least one witch's death, but I have not slept or eaten a decent meal in over twenty-four hours. On top of that quagmire, I was written up today and threatened with dismissal for being late. You know why I was late? Because I was poisoned by a goblin and almost bled to death. A girl *has* to take a shower after that, Poe."

"You could be fired?" Poe fluffed his feathers in alarm.

"Yes, and if I am, I can't take care of you in the manner you've grown accustomed. Sure, the house is paid for, but there is the problem of food and heat. It wouldn't be such a big deal if I'd married Rick as planned. He had quite the nest egg. But as that plan is on permanent hiatus, I need this job. Only, I can't take a night off because Rick can't shift or do magic to defend the ward." I ran out of breath near the end of my tirade and had to take a long and noisy inhale. Once oxygen was accounted for, I banged my head against the arm of the sofa.

"Special delivery!" I looked toward the open door to see Logan staring openmouthed at my headbanging. The Valentine burger I'd ordered on the way home was in a brown paper bag in his hands.

"Why do you look like someone just died?" he asked.

"It was her father," Poe said without hesitation.

All the blood drained from Logan's face, and he dropped the bag.

"Poe is being an asshole. My father is alive and well. I'm upset because I almost got fired today."

"And she almost died last night," Poe added.

I waved my hand in the air. "That too. Near death, bloody battle, blah, blah, blah. You've heard it all before." I stood and retrieved my dinner from the floor. "Thanks for bringing this. You have no idea the fucking day I've had."

"Geesh, language, Grateful. There are ravens who act like children in the room." Logan shot Poe an angry glance. "Now, tell Uncle Logan what happened."

I kicked the door closed behind him. "Okay. Come in. Sit down. I gotta eat, and we are definitely going to need wine for this."

* * * * *

Two bottles later, Logan stared across the table at me in speechless pity. "What are you going to do?" he asked in a stage whisper, as if Hecate was in the next room. "What if it *is* the goddess? How do you defend yourself against a goddess?"

"I don't know." I rested my cheek on the table. The wood was blissfully cool, and I contemplated taking a nap, despite the awkward position. "What if it's not her and I have a group of deadly goblins after me for their own reasons? Let me tell you, the asshat with the bow and arrow was very hard to kill. I don't know, maybe I was just weak from lack of Rick, but it was like my magic fizzled in his presence. I've never had that happen."

"If it was goblin magic and not the absence of Tall, Dark, and Brooding, maybe Soleil can shed some light on the subject for you. She's been around for a while."

I laughed once, then again, and then the laughs kept coming until I sounded like a machine gun. "Shed some light," I said, resting my forehead on my fists. "You said a celestial fae who bleeds sunlight could 'shed some light' on the subject."

Logan looked at me with a straight face. "You are slaphappy."

I was about to agree when there was a knock at the door. With a groan, I lifted my head and pushed off the table to drag my aching limbs to the door. Polina stood under my porch light in a fitted blue gown that reminded me of Cinderella's. Her red hair was tied up in a neat chignon. She even held a magic wand with a gigantic crystal on the end in her right hand.

"You look like a princess," I said.

"You look like someone died." She scanned my dirty scrubs.

I frowned and opened the door wider. "No one died. Just a terrible day and not getting any better."

"You'll have to invite me in. Your protective ward is making me itch even from here."

"Polina, I invite you into my home," I said, relieved the spells I kept on the house were working as planned, even in my weakened state.

She smiled and stepped over the threshold. "That's better."

The large leather satchel hanging from her shoulder looked weighted down, like she had something heavy inside. "Did you bring a bowling ball to sacrifice?" I chuckled, feeling quite witty.

Polina didn't laugh. In fact, she seemed distracted. I followed her line of sight directly to Logan, whose expression could also be described as distracted. "Oh, sorry, I'm being rude," I said. "Polina, this is my good friend Logan. Logan, this is Polina. She's a metal witch who has been helping me."

No one moved a muscle. I glanced between them, wondering what I'd missed. Both looked positively pallid.

"Do you two know each other or something?" I asked.

Polina cleared her throat and shook her head. A blush stained her cheeks on either side of a slight smile. "No. Um, Logan, it's very nice to meet you." She took a step and extended her hand.

Logan wrapped his fingers around hers and pumped her arm dumbly before giving his own head a shake. He thumped his noggin a few times with the heel of his hand. "Sorry. You do seem familiar to me. Do you ever come into Valentine's?"

Teeth gleaming, Polina answered, "No. I've been, er, buried for most of the last year."

"Oh, I know how that can be," Logan said. "The hours I work at the restaurant are crazy too."

Did he just wink? They were still holding hands. Ooookay. "Um, Polina, I need to get cleaned up before we start." I pointed at my scrubs. "Do you mind waiting down here for a few minutes? Maybe Logan can keep you company."

Logan's distraction melted into confusion, then concern. He retracted his hand from Polina's grip. "Actually, I…" He scratched the back of his head. "Ah, it's getting late. I better hit the road." He tossed his thumb over his shoulder toward the door.

Out of the corner of my eye, I saw Polina's face fall. She recovered quickly. "It was good to meet you, Logan."

"Uh, you too."

"Thanks for listening tonight," I said, pulling him into a hug.

"What are friends for?" With a smile and a small wave, he was out the door.

I was turning the lock when Polina asked, "What is he?"

"Human," I said. "A talented human. He's a medium. Can speak to the dead. Mostly his mother. She seems to be his psychic spirit of choice anyway. Why?"

She frowned. "Human, you say? He has a quality…" She circled a hand in front of her chest. After a moment, she gave up on finding the right word and dropped her arm to her side. "I thought he was something more."

"Nope. That's it, a human medium. Oh, and Tabetha totally fucked with his head. He fears the witchy world. I try to keep him out of it as much as possible." I wasn't stupid or blind. The flash of attraction between them was obvious. But Polina was all wrong for Logan, and he knew it. It was best to make that as clear as possible. "I need a cup of coffee and a shower or this isn't going to happen. Would you like one? Coffee, that is. You don't look in need of a shower."

"No, thank you. But I would like to get started. The spell takes time."

"Poe!" I screamed toward the ceiling.

Polina jumped back, grabbing the base of her neck at my outburst. It couldn't be helped. I was not climbing the stairs unnecessarily.

My familiar swooped down from the second floor and landed on the banister.

"You don't have to yell," Poe said. "I have very good hearing."

"Please show Polina to the attic. I'll be up in just a moment."

Poe bobbed his head and took flight. Polina lifted her skirts to jog up the stairs after him.

CHAPTER 7
Gold Dust Woman

Later, fully caffeinated and smelling less like hospital, I joined Polina in my attic. It occurred to me that the level of trust I had in Polina was extreme and perhaps chancy. I'd invited her into my home and given her unsupervised access to the attic, my most personal and sacred space. My faith in her wasn't founded on guarantees or sorcery but on good old-fashioned gut instinct. Then again, our short friendship was built on high stakes. I'd dug her out of the ground at Tabetha's. She'd saved me from binding with Julius last night and brought me to Rick to be healed. I'd found out she'd also created my magic mirror. We had a history, in this life and the last, and I trusted her.

While I'd been freshening up, Polina had drawn three concentric circles on the sanded wood floor using gold dust. At the center of the circle, a crystal ball was positioned on a metal stand in the shape of a dragon's foot. It was the typical, theatrical kind of crystal ball gypsies everywhere used to tell the future. Only, the magic coming off this orb was far from make-believe. It raised the hair on my arms and made my left eye twitch.

"This looks complicated," I said.

"It is. I started this spell when I left your caretaker's home. The preparation was grueling, but I think it's finally ready."

"Last time I crossed over to talk to Mommy dearest, I offered some coffee and wine as a sacrifice. Wham, bam, I went over. Why so much effort?"

"We need to present a united front to Mother and be prepared for anything. We don't know what we are getting ourselves into. The orb is leaded glass. A little blood and it will take both of us where we want to go, together."

"And the circles?"

"A type of clock or timer. The moment we go over, the inner circle will ignite. If it burns a complete revolution, the fire will jump to the next ring and the next. I've measured it out to give us one hour, although time in Mother's world can feel different than ours. Once the last ring burns to completion, its enchantment will pull our souls back into our bodies."

I pinched my eyebrows together. "Do you think we'll need that? I mean, I thought we established that if Mother wanted me dead, she could do it in a heartbeat. If she hasn't killed me yet, why would she kill me on the other side?"

Polina rubbed her palms together in nervous circles. "I didn't want to worry you, but I've heard our mother has a proclivity for indirect means. For example, she didn't kill Tabetha herself; she gave you permission to kill Tabetha."

"More of a reason to believe I'm safe in her presence."

"Hecate is the goddess of crossroads. We could find ourselves in an endless labyrinth or tangled in a massive spider's web."

I remembered Mother's jungle and the snake that coiled about her arms. "I see your point. Thank you for the spell."

"It's a strong one. We're drawing on three elements here. Your attic for air, the floor for wood, and my orb for metal. The two of us together are quite powerful. I hope she takes us seriously."

I hugged myself, catching a chill. "Uh, Polina?"

"Yeah."

"Do you think it's wise to look powerful in front of Mother? In the past, I've found it's best to be as unassuming as possible in her presence. If she's pissed I'm housing two elements, won't she be threatened that we're using three?"

"Right." She tapped her cheek. "We'll stress your almost-death and my recovery from being fertilizer. She loves misery. We will go for the groveling angle—throw ourselves on her mercy and beg for her guidance."

"Angle? Sounds like an accurate assessment of what we are doing to me," I said, raising an eyebrow.

Polina tiptoed carefully into the center circle and took a seat in front of the orb. "Come on in, but be careful not to upset the rings."

Step by shaky step, I picked my way into the circle without disrupting the rings of gold dust and lowered myself to the floor, sitting cross-legged across the orb from her. My skin tingled with the magic bouncing between us.

"Do you feel that?" she asked.

If I hadn't felt it, I could see it. Her hair had come loose from its bun and floated around her head as if she was submerged in water. "Yeah. Everything tingles." A lock of my blonde hair drifted to eye level. My body was wickedly light, suspended in soupy magic. "How do we do this?"

"Blood. I've got it covered." She retrieved her wand from inside the neck of her dress. "I keep her next to my heart."

"Smart."

"Place your hands on the orb."

I did as she asked, placing my spread fingers on either side of the crystal ball. She gripped the jeweled tip of her wand in her fist and dragged it out slowly, slicing the skin of her palm. Blood pooled at the heel of her hand, then dripped onto the orb where a recess in the top of the crystal caught the drop and channeled it inside the sphere.

The ruby red sank and spread, veining out from the center and swirling in the magic of the leaded glass between my hands. It was beautiful and horrifying, light pulsing behind magnified red blood cells, a glass heart beating beneath my fingertips. Heat radiated from the orb, warming my face, and then a flash of light blinded me. I ascended from the floor, spinning until my legs flung out from under me. I gripped the orb for dear life. From one world into the next, my heart hammered in my throat, and I panted through the surge of power.

We skidded to a stop on a stretch of thick moss, the orb disappearing from our grip. Next to me, Polina pushed herself onto one hip. We were under a canopy of green. Hecate's garden.

"We made it," I said excitedly. Polina did not share my enthusiasm. She stared over my shoulder, her face a ghastly pale color. I followed her stare, rising and turning in place.

"Welcome, my children." Hecate's voice reverberated in the greenery around us. "What brings you to my domain?"

CHAPTER 8
Mother

Being in the presence of Hecate was always disorienting. She moved like a rattlesnake's tail, her three forms distorting with her power, alternating forward placement of each aspect—maiden, mother, or crone. I repeatedly blinked in a vain attempt to focus, but the problem wasn't the clarity of my vision. The force that was my goddess mother sifted through me and weighed my soul before taking the form of the mother figure. Her long dark hair cascaded over one shoulder of a sheer toga that left nothing to the imagination.

"Mother," I said by way of greeting. "We need your help."

She glanced between the two of us, then reached her hand to the branches above her head. A thick yellow snake coiled around her arm and slithered across her shoulders. "I can't imagine why you'd need *my* help, Grateful Knight.

Two elements reside inside you and a third stands in support of you." She bared her teeth as she stroked the snake's head. "As I recall, your caretaker holds dominion over a fourth."

"Rick, er, my caretaker is sick. He can't remember how to use his power." I spread my hands in exasperation. "Look, I'd be happy to give Tabetha's element away. You can have it. I don't want it."

Her eyes widened. "Is that so? I seem to remember you signing the scroll to accept the power." The snake raised its head and hissed in my direction.

"I… I had to! I needed Tabetha's spellbook to save Rick."

Behind me, Polina cleared her throat in warning. "Grateful has made a terrible mistake signing for Tabetha's grimoire. If there were a way to undo the deed, she would perform the task forthwith."

Damn, Polina was good at this. No questions, just putting it out there for the goddess to contemplate.

Hecate stroked the snake's head rhythmically. "My dear Polina. Always the trusting witch. Don't you remember how things began with Tabetha? Already the power corrupts Grateful's soul. Air corrodes metal, my dear. Be cautious what alliances you make."

I whispered to Polina, "I would never hurt you."

The goddess cackled wickedly. "Don't make promises you can't keep, daughter."

"I never wanted the power!" I insisted. "I just wanted a way to set things right with Rick. Tell me how to get my life back."

She took an inhumanly graceful step closer until my skin hurt from the energy that radiated from her. "But you see, my dear, whether or not you wanted it, you have the power, and there is only one way to be rid of it."

"Tell me. I'll do anything."

She raised an eyebrow. "A witch who unites all five elements has power enough to do almost anything. As much power as me, it is said. She could cast any or all of her elemental powers out of herself. In fact, such a witch can undo even the most permanent of spells. I should warn you, such a feat has never been accomplished. Any witch who has ever tried has met Tabetha's end. Other witches are not keen on allowing the union of elements, nor am I. After all, what witch would gain such power only to cast it aside?"

"Me," I said. "I would."

Hecate laughed and narrowed her eyes. "One who united the elements could even challenge me. Do you wish to challenge me, Grateful?" Her cool voice rippled evenly through the space between us.

"O-of course not," I said. "I don't want to be you. I don't want more power. I just want to be rid of Tabetha's element and manage my ward in peace."

"Is that why you bound a vampire to yourself?" Hecate hissed. "A strange step to take for a witch who believes she has too much power."

What? How did she even know that?

"He drank my blood. I didn't know. I didn't do it on purpose."

"I didn't know," Hecate imitated sarcastically. "Such a fool you claim to be. As foolish as a fox. I know better, daughter. You are as benevolent as a scorpion, a poisonous pest to be squashed under heel." The two torches on either side of her stone door flamed to life.

Was she moving for the door? Leaving us? I couldn't let her go. I had to know the truth. "Did you send a goblin to try to kill me?" I blurted. Polina audibly inhaled. Above me, the sky exploded with thunder and lightning. I ducked my head from fear of being struck down.

"How dare you!" Hecate bellowed. Two gigantic black dogs appeared beside her, their growling heads drooling and snapping at me. The door behind her opened, and she backed toward it.

Polina elbowed me in the side, hard. "No questions, Grateful."

I couldn't keep my big, fat mouth shut. It didn't make any sense to me. If she was such a threat, why was she backing away? If she wanted me dead, why didn't she kill me now?

"You want me dead, but you can't kill me yourself," I said. "There's some reason you can't hurt me directly."

A roar between a growl and a scream parted her lips, and her pupils shattered, her eyes filling with bright red light. "Do not tell me what I can or cannot do, witch."

She pointed at my chest. "*Dínọ tịn ádeiá!*" A red column of fire flew from her hand and hit me between the breasts.

Pain channeled through me, crushing my spine. I screamed and thrashed my arms at my sides as the smell of my burning flesh stung my nostrils. Had she blown a hole right through me? With a sharp withdrawal of her hand, she pulled me toward her, tractor-beam style.

"Polina!" I cried, but what could she do?

When the goddess let me go, I found myself with her, on the wrong side of the door, panting and wet with perspiration, but still breathing. I clutched my throbbing chest and turned my head to stare at Polina through the open door. Her eyes widened, and she covered her mouth with her hands in horror. The stone slammed shut between us.

Quivering with fear, I instinctively reached for Nightshade. Not there. I'd been wearing her, but she must not have passed into this realm.

Hecate peeled her lips back from her teeth, stroking the heads of the hellhounds at her side. "Do you wish to challenge me, Grateful Knight? If you do, survive to reach the center of the labyrinth and prove yourself worthy." She dissolved into the shadows.

The dogs remained, heads low and ears back. They stalked me as I backed away slowly, both hands raised in front of me. "Good doggie. Easy. I like dogs, really."

The beasts did not return my feigned affection. They attacked. I crossed my arms in front of my head to protect my face. Claws scraped through my flesh, and teeth sank into my head. I struggled, pounding my fists and kicking away the dogs' claws. Then, a miracle. An invisible force yanked me backward by the waist.

I crumpled into the fetal position, the world swirling around me in a disorienting array of color and light. Gold dust scattered as I slid into my attic, knocking the crystal ball off its pedestal. It rolled across the floor into Polina's shaking hands.

Disoriented, I raised my arms, finding them bloody. The flesh was shredded and the bright red drip cruising down my nose was indication that my head wounds were similarly real.

"I'll get Rick," Poe said from his perch near the window. He took flight out the pet door before I passed out again.

* * * * *

"You need me," Rick said.

I opened my eyes to find him sitting on the side of my bed with Nightshade in hand. Behind him, Poe nested in one of my T-shirts on the dresser, his raven eyes fixated on me. Polina waited nearby, her hands folded in front of her hips. Other than her hair coming loose from its bun, she still looked fresh and princess-like.

"You're lucky to be alive. Those wounds won't heal on their own." Polina nodded toward Rick.

"Come, drink." Rick scored his wrist with Nightshade and brought it to my lips.

I didn't wait for an invitation. I latched on to his wrist.

"Now that I know you're not dying," Polina said, voice shrill, "I am going to kill you! Do you have a brain in your blonde skull? You could have gotten us both killed. What the hell were you thinking, taunting Hecate like that?"

I broke from Rick and sat up to respond, although I cradled his arm in my lap in case I needed more. "I wanted to learn her limitations."

"She's a goddess; she has no limitations." Polina tossed her hands up.

Poe bobbed his head. "I have to agree with Polina on this one. Hecate could strike you down at any time."

"No. I don't think she can."

Every eye in the room fixated on me. "She obviously wants me dead. She blasted a ray of energy through my chest." I pulled the neck of my shirt down to reveal a scabby burn mark. "If it were possible for her to kill me directly, she would have."

"Do you know that for sure, or are you speculating?" Poe asked.

"It's an educated guess. When she pulled me into her labyrinth, she said I could challenge her if I reached the center. Why? Why couldn't I challenge her in the jungle? Behind the door? And then it occurred to me that she must have rules of engagement."

"Rules," Polina said, hands on her hips. "You believe the goddess has limitations, and you felt it was your duty to test them out at the possible expense of my life?"

"I'm sorry. I didn't mean to put you at risk, but she admitted as much to us. She said if a witch collected all five elements it would make her as powerful as Hecate—powerful enough to challenge her for her role."

Polina nodded. "You're right; she did. She also said no one who tried has ever succeeded or lived to tell the tale."

"She invited me to challenge her today because she knew I would lose. In fact, without your spell to draw me back into my body, I'd probably have died in that labyrinth." I laced my fingers into Rick's, and he didn't pull away. His touch was comforting.

"Grateful, do you even remember why we went to see her today?"

I shrugged. "To see if she knew who was behind the Goblin Trinate's attack."

She squinted at me. "And did we learn the answer to that question?"

I rolled the conversation through my head. "Um. No."

Polina held up one finger. "Exactly! However, we did learn one undeniable truth."

"What?"

"Whether or not she can do it herself, after today, Mother definitely wants you dead."

"Crap." My gaze darted from Poe to Rick, but no one disagreed with Polina's statement.

Polina gathered her bag from the floor near her feet and headed for the door. "If I were you, I'd put my affairs in order."

CHAPTER 9
Invitations

It must have been around two a.m. when Polina walked out. I didn't blame her for being angry. When I pissed off Mother, it put her at risk as well. She was my only witch friend, and I deeply regretted that my actions might cause her misery. Did they make an edible bouquet for this occasion? *Sorry for risking your life. Have some chocolate-covered pineapple.*

"Would you mind?" Poe said, tapping at the window with his beak. "All of this drama has made me hungry."

"You could fly out your door in the attic."

"Or you could get off your *arse* and open the window for me."

I flipped him off, but Rick complied, sliding the chipped-paint frame on its track just high enough to allow Poe out.

"You shouldn't give in to him like that," I said, standing to grab a set of pajamas from my drawer. "You'll spoil him."

"You need your rest. If I had not let him out, you would still be fighting about it."

Rick was right. I'd been up for more than twenty-four hours and was nearing collapse. I hastened into the bathroom to rinse off the bloody remains of my battle with Hecate before bed. "Would you like to stay?" I called through the door.

He cleared his throat before answering. "I am becoming accustomed to my lack of need for sleep. I fear I would keep you up. I'll show myself out." I heard my door close behind him as he left.

I didn't take it personally; I was too exhausted to mind. As soon as I was clean and in my most comfortable pajamas, I crawled into bed and drifted into a dead, dreamless sleep.

For a painfully inadequate amount of time.

With a start, I awoke to find a dark figure standing over me. A familiar dark figure. One I'd like to decapitate for waking me before dawn.

"Gary, what the hell are you doing in my bedroom?" I snapped.

"Julius sent me. I tried to knock, but no one answered."

"No one answered because it's the middle of the night."

"Early morning, actually." He shifted from foot to foot, glancing toward the window. "It's an emergency."

"What kind of emergency would warrant you using my coerced invitation from last winter to enter my locked home?"

"The Goblin Trinate is in Carlton City. They're tracking you, Grateful. They'll be here at any moment."

I sat up in bed. "You are shitting me. Do not shit me about this, Gary. It's not funny."

"I'm not shitting you!" he insisted. "Julius is prepared to offer you his safe house, but you've got to come with me now. The sun is rising. We'll barely make it before dawn."

Gary moved to the window in a flash. "Uh-oh."

"What?" I scrambled off the bed.

Gary pointed toward the tree line across the road from my house. "There, in the forest." Pinpoints of silver glinted in the moonlight and platinum hair flashed and floated between the trees. Goblins.

"Fuck."

Just then, a flurry of black appeared and pounded the glass. Gary disappeared from my side at super speed. I moved into the space he vacated and propped open the window. "It's okay, Gary. It's just my familiar being an asshole, as usual." Poe swooped into the room and landed on my dresser.

A hiss came from above my head. Gary was hanging by his fingernails from the ceiling but dropped to my side when he saw it was Poe.

"You startle easily for an undead," I said cynically.

He smoothed his button-down shirt. "Well, er, yes. I suppose I do."

"I'll pretend not to notice your ex-boyfriend is in your bedroom and get down to business," Poe interrupted. "The Goblin Trinate have surrounded our home."

I dug my hands into my hair. "This sucks, but there's no need to panic. We're safe here. My protective spells are in place. They can't get in. I'll call our supernatural detective extraordinaire, Silas, and have them arrested."

I grabbed my phone off the nightstand. If anyone could figure out how to shake these guys, it was Silas.

"Do your spells cover goblins?" Gary asked. "Julius warned me they might be resistant to your magic. Something about their blood."

Poe swiveled his head on his neck as only birds can do and searched the darkness outside the window. Streaks of platinum crossed the road and flashed up my driveway. "We're about to find out."

Each of us held our breath as the rattle of the front doorknob reached us. There was a sharp crack and a familiar squeal of hinges. "Holy crow," I whispered. "They're in."

I grabbed Nightshade from the place I kept her under my pillow and strapped her to my back before I shoved my cell phone into my back pocket. Motioning with my hand for Poe and Gary to follow, I slipped into the hall and up the stairs to the attic. Once everyone was inside my most magical space, I locked it behind me. I conjured a large wardrobe to block the entrance. "It will only last until sunrise," I said.

"That makes two of us." Gary fidgeted near the window.

Poe flapped his wings and landed on the windowsill near his pet door. "What now? That won't hold them for long, and there's no way out unless you plan to sprout wings."

I raised one incredulous eyebrow in Gary's direction. "Aren't you supposed to be rescuing me? If you don't know how to stop the goblins, why did Julius send you? If he was worried about me and wanted me to come to his safe house, he should have come himself."

Gary tilted his head and looked at me like I was stupid. "He can't get into your house, Grateful. If you needed rescuing, he'd be helpless."

"So... now she needs to rescue you, as well as herself," Poe snapped. "Make sure to thank Julius for that."

Gary flipped him the finger.

"This isn't helping, you two." I crossed the attic to the *The Book of Light* and *Copse Magicum*, Forest Magic, my two magical grimoires. Truth was, I didn't have a clue what to do next. I could climb out the window, but then what? "Wings," I said, frantically flipping pages. "You're a genius, Poe. We need to fly out of here."

"You've flown before," Poe said. "I've seen you hover."

"I can hover, but I don't have enough control. Not good enough to call it flying."

"They have arrows," Gary reminded. Hovering was not going to cut it. I needed to fly or I'd be target practice.

I lifted Tabetha's magic wand from next to *Copse Magicum*. I'd resisted trying to use it in the past; it held bad memories for me. However, an idea was working its way to the front of my brain. It was a long shot, but maybe my only shot.

"When I hover, I have to concentrate on pushing the air away from myself to propel from the ground. What if I sat on a magical object and concentrated on lifting that object using the air around me?"

Poe rolled his eyes. "Like a broom? How cliché."

"Not a broom. A branch." I held up the crooked wand that used to be Tabetha's and concentrated. It extended to the length of my body, sprouting a few leafy segments as it grew. With a little effort, I levitated the branch and sent it soaring around the attic. When it returned to me, I climbed on, sidesaddle, and floated across the wood floor to the window.

"I don't get it," Gary said. "How is levitating a branch easier than levitating yourself?"

"The power comes from me," I said evenly, trying to hold steady. "This gives me a consistent place to direct my concentrated effort."

Gary frowned. "That makes no physical or mechanical sense."

I shrugged. "Maybe not, but it's the best I've got. Gary, you jump down and distract them. Poe, stay close and help me focus my magic."

"Got it," Poe said.

Behind us, the door rattled. I motioned for Gary to open the window. He complied.

"Meet me where I was turned," the vampire whispered, so quietly I had to read his lips. I nodded. He'd told me the story of Anna Bathory turning him months ago. I knew the place.

In one lithe move, he leaped from the window into the oak tree in my front yard, then onto the road, racing toward the woods. A single streak of platinum followed him. Hmmm. Not much of a distraction. The door to the attic cracked against the wardrobe behind me. I kicked off, folding myself to the branch to fit through the window.

My flight wasn't nearly as graceful as I'd hoped. I jerked forward and side to side like a turbulent airplane. As I struggled to hold myself aloft, Poe glided nervously near my head. "Steady," he whispered. "Don't draw attention."

"I'm trying," I whispered. I succeeded in driving forward in one awkward thrust toward the stone bridge between my house and Rick's. If I could make it to his place, I could borrow his car to escape.

An arrow whizzed past my ear. "Watch out," I cried to Poe, looking over my shoulder. A sea of platinum heads had formed at the end of my driveway. The twang of drawn bows left me desperate to propel forward, but I lurched and stopped in frustrating bursts.

"Pointy-eared sons of bitches," Poe cursed.

"Go. Go," I said to Poe. "They'll skewer you like a pheasant. Find me later."

My familiar nodded and left me, soaring like a bullet toward Monk's Hill Cemetery. Smart bird. No way would the goblins risk entering my hellmouth.

I changed course to follow him, but another round of arrows cut me off. Without Poe's presence amplifying my magic, my control faltered. I dove and rolled, almost falling off the branch. Distracted, I dropped like a rock toward the pavement. The arrows cut through my hair, just missing my scalp. I landed on the bridge, breaking my fall with a desperate gust of wind that wasn't enough to keep me from tumbling into the stone railing.

On quick and silent feet, the goblins left the end of my drive to pursue me. I sprinted for Rick's. A silver arrow hit the road near my feet. I was too exposed on the bridge, but unless I threw myself over the side of it, there was nowhere else to go. Halfway across, the squeal of tires and approaching headlights forced me to scramble out of the way. I slammed into the wall to keep from becoming road kill.

Blinded by the headlights, I heard the screech of braking tires, and pebbles sprayed against my calves. The car stopped in front of me and the passenger door flew open.

"Get in!" Rick commanded.

Breathless, I dove into the leather seat headfirst, transforming the branch back into a wand as quickly as I

could. Another barrage of silver arrows rained around us,
impaling the hood of the Tesla. Rick threw the car into
reverse and slammed on the accelerator, wheels spinning
before jerking us backward off the bridge. A hair-raising
three-point turn later, I was able to get upright, hook my
hand into the passenger door, and slam it closed. A silver
arrow crashed through my window, impaling the back of
my headrest.

"When did you learn to drive?" I yelled to Rick.

"Tonight!" He floored the accelerator.

"What? How?"

"I Googled it!" More arrows pinged against the road
behind us, but the Tesla was burning rubber out of Red
Grove.

"When did you learn how to use Google?" I asked,
staring at the mob of goblins growing more distant behind
us.

"After you bought me the laptop," he said.

I stared at his profile, the wind filtering through the
broken window behind me and blowing my hair into my
face. I gathered it in my hands and stared at him in awe.
Had I underestimated Rick? Memory or not, he wasn't
helpless. He blew both stop signs on the way out of town,
and I glanced nervously at the dash to find the
speedometer topping a hundred.

"Don't take this the wrong way, but I think you
should let me drive," I said.

He turned sharp gray eyes on me and flashed an
unruly smile. "Not a chance."

* * * * *

We arrived at the alley behind the Mill Wheel just before dawn. Gary motioned for us to pull the Tesla into one of those twenty-minute oil change places across the street. A group of vampires closed the garage door behind us. As soon as we were out of the vehicle, they covered the Tesla with a tarp

"This way," Gary said. He unlocked a door in the back and held it open for me.

Against my better judgment, I squeezed past him and descended into a musty stone stairwell. Rick followed, pressing into my side and lacing his fingers into mine. I liked the handholding. Not only did it show a level of trust on his part, but there was a sense of protective instinct in the gesture. Rick was watching out for me. Hell, Rick had saved my ass tonight. My heart swelled.

When Gary closed the door, the darkness was absolute. I lifted my hand and blew against my palm, igniting a tiny blue flame.

"It's too dangerous," Gary said. He bent my fingers to close my hand, effectively extinguishing my magic. "Light carries, and magic light is detectable by other means."

"I can't see in the dark," I said.

Rick tucked his arm under mine. "I can," he whispered.

I turned my face toward his voice and hugged his arm to my chest. "Okay. Gary, lead the way."

We descended into a passageway of darkness. Rick guided me, holding me up by the waist as I tripped on the uneven floor. "What is this place?" I asked.

"Prohibition tunnels. They were built in 1923 to aid in the smuggling of alcohol between the Carlton City speakeasies."

"I'm surprised they're still sound. Is the roof going to collapse on my head?" I asked.

"No. They've been maintained. They're used today by my kind to get around during the day. Humans who come down here these days are usually lunch."

"Nice," I said flatly.

"Not to worry; you are under Julius's protection. Your blood must be one hell of a treat. He's threatened all of us with a thousand years in a silver-lined box if anyone damages a hair on your head. No vamp would dare touch you."

I jumped when something scurried across my toes.

"Do not worry, Grateful. It was only a rat," Rick whispered into my ear.

"That's comforting."

"This way," Gary said.

Rick turned me by the shoulders. "There is a stairway. Allow me to help you."

Before I could say a word, Rick swept me into his arms and jogged up the flight of steps. At the top, Gary opened another door. Jovial music, voices, and warm light flooded over us. I blinked to adjust my vision while Rick set me down.

Beyond a short corridor, I stood at the threshold of a grand speakeasy, windowless, as I'd expected a vampire bar to be, and furnished in dark wood, red velvet, and brass. The bartender wore suspenders and a bow tie in the 1920's fashion. Waitresses buzzed between round tables at super speed in flapper dresses, stained-glass votives lighting their way. In the back, males and females danced to jazz music on a small dance floor. Most were vampires. A few were human.

Heads turned as we entered. Seated couples looked up from their drinks, and a few vampires paused their dancing to flash fang my direction. Vampire after vampire glared at me. I bristled, but no one backed up their threatening looks.

"What's their problem?" I asked.

"It's not what you think. It's not because you're a witch," Gary said matter-of-factly. "Although, I'd ask you to keep your blade stashed. We don't want to cause a panic."

"Why are they all pissy?"

He paused and spread his hands. "You're underdressed. There's a dress code."

I looked down at myself. I was still wearing my plaid sleep shorts and a T-shirt sporting a picture of a sock monkey with the caption *Nice Banana*. I ran my thumbs under the straps to the sheath on my back that held

Nightshade. My face felt warm. "Uh. Do you have something more appropriate for me to wear?"

Gary grimaced.

"He doesn't, but I do." From the shadows, Julius's radiant blue eyes became visible before the rest of him. He melded into the dim light and lifted his rocks glass of scotch in a little toast to me. "Pleasure to see you again, Miss Knight. I am relieved to learn that Gary got you out in one piece, although I don't recall inviting the sidekick." He glanced pointedly at Rick.

"Rick goes where I go."

"Perhaps your caretaker can wait at the bar while you and I discuss business."

I frowned. "What business do we need to discuss without my caretaker?"

"For starters, why the Goblin Trinate want you dead and how long you will need sanctuary in my safe house."

When he put it that way, I did owe him something for saving me. My shoulders softened, and the vampire held out his hand, bowing slightly at the waist. Julius was ancient. I wasn't sure how ancient, but I suspected he held a wealth of information about my new enemies.

I looked at Rick and motioned with my chin toward the bar. "Give me a minute?"

He nodded once and released my arm to do as I asked.

Once he was gone, I slipped my hand into Julius's and allowed the vampire to lead me from the room.

CHAPTER 10
The Safe House

Julius guided me to the back of the speakeasy and up a flight of stairs to a wood-paneled hallway. The second door on the left opened into an expansive bedroom that reminded me of something from *The Great Gatsby*. The four-poster bed at the center struck me as larger than life, a piece of furniture of inhuman standards with red silk sheets and a velvet comforter. Clearly, the bed was meant to be the centerpiece of the room, but that was hardly the most impressive feature. The two-story walls were lined with books, old and new, with a sliding brass ladder attached to the shelves to ensure each of them was accessible. Along one wall, a break in the shelving allowed for a fireplace where a lively fire crackled and popped. Two oversized red velvet chairs hugged its warmth. I took one look at their plush cushions and curved backs and sagged with exhaustion.

"You need sleep," Julius said. "You're safe here. I'll watch over you. Rest a few hours." He gestured toward the bed.

I ran a hand through my bedhead and rubbed my sleepy eyes. "Eh, no, thanks."

"A drink perhaps? While we talk?"

I nodded. He disappeared behind the massive bed, and soon I heard the clink of ice against glass and the slosh of pouring liquid.

"What do you know about the Goblin Trinate?" I asked.

He emerged from behind the headboard and handed me a scotch on the rocks. With a crook of his head, he led the way to the fire and folded himself into one of the red chairs facing it. "Join me," he said. From my vantage point, all I could see was his foot draped across one knee and the scotch glass in his perfectly manicured hand on the armrest.

I hesitated. I was afraid if I sat in the cozy chair, I wouldn't get up again. But Julius had information I needed, and I was exhausted. If I didn't sit down, I would fall down. I joined him in the second red chair, curling my legs beneath me.

"Better?" He gave me a toothy grin. "The Goblin Trinate consists of masters of organized crime. They adore wealth and power and will do almost anything for the right price. Human precepts of morality are foreign to them, although they are usually neutral when it comes to other supernatural entities."

"So, why do they want me dead?"

Julius sipped his scotch thoughtfully. "I don't think it is the goblins. I fear your intended demise was the work of another witch, one who has potentially given them protection from your magic."

"Nightshade's magic was useless against them. I wasn't able to judge the goblin. Believe me, I tried."

"Another witch's involvement would explain their sudden interest in you, your inability to sentence your attacker, and how they knew exactly where you would be. Perhaps a friend of Tabetha's?"

I swirled the scotch in my glass, watching the ice cut through the thick amber liquid. I needed a drink, but I held off, worried the alcohol would make me too tired to think. "Or Mommy dearest," I murmured under my breath.

The vampire froze. "Are you suggesting that the goddess Hecate might be behind the attack?"

"You heard that?"

He rolled his eyes. "I'm a vampire. I can hear what the woman at the bar downstairs is ordering."

"You might as well know what you're up against housing me here. Hecate may have given the impression tonight that she, um, might, maybe, want me dead." I shifted my bottom lip to the side and shrugged as if being on the goddess's hit list was a stroke of bad luck similar to missing the bus or running out of change at the Laundromat.

Julius narrowed his eyes at me. "Why?"

"She's not happy that I accepted Tabetha's grimoire in order to save Rick. I can control two elements—*control* being a generous word since I can't even stop the roses on my banister from growing."

He rubbed a small circle over one temple, peering at me through the corner of his eye. "Can you undo what you've done?"

"That's the rub," I said, straightening in my chair. "Hecate said the only way to complete a spell strong enough to remove the extra element is to unite all of the elements and then cast off the extra ones." I sighed heavily. "Apparently, this would give me almost unlimited power, enough to potentially challenge Hecate herself. And, of course, the goddess does not believe that anyone would unite the elements just to get rid of them."

Julius snorted. "Of course not. Who would?"

"I would." I threw up my hands. "I just want my life back. I don't want to be a goddess." I swirled the scotch in my glass again, raising it to my lips, but lowering it before taking a sip. "Julius, you've been around for, what, a few hundred years, right?"

Pensively, he leaned his elbows on his knees. "Over two thousand now."

"Two thousand years! Holy crow! When were you born?"

His blue eyes darkened, and he leaned back in his chair. "As rude as that question is, I find myself compelled to answer. Perhaps the bond I have to you means I must. My parents named me after Julius Caesar. I was born in

Rome in the year 42 BC and turned to eternal life in 12 BC."

"Whoa. You're thirty years old forever?"

"Twenty-nine. I was turned five days before my thirtieth birthday, but who's counting?"

"Twelve BC! The things you must've seen." I stared at him in amazement. "Did you know Jesus?"

"Not personally, and not as well as I would have liked," he murmured. "I beseech you, I'm compelled to answer your questions but you must know this inquiry into my past is acutely painful. Vampires do not enjoy talking about the passage of time." His lips pursed, and he stared into the fire.

My face fell. No matter what power I had over Julius, what type of person would I be if I made his pain my entertainment? "Sorry. As I was saying, have you ever heard of any other way for a witch to cast off elemental power other than uniting the elements?"

"No," he said quickly. "The closest thing I can think of is the creation of a caretaker. That particular spell gives a human a witch's immortality but not her elemental power, although the spell imparts a new elemental power onto her caretaker."

"Crap. I was afraid you'd say that."

"Perhaps if you bound yourself to me?" Julius suggested.

I grimaced and looked him in the eye. "Julius, let's make something clear. You will not attempt to bind me or to feed me your blood without my permission."

He shot up from his chair and grabbed the glass out of my hand.

"I'm not done with that," I said.

"The ice has melted. I'll bring you a fresh one." He crossed the room to the bar again. "I have a confession to make."

"Okay."

"The night I rescued you from Bathory, I had no intention of drinking your blood." He returned to my side and handed me a fresh scotch. When I took the glass, his long, icy fingers brushed against mine. I shivered. It was a tangible reminder that he was an animated corpse.

"Then why did you?" I asked, taking a drink.

"Your blood sings to me. That night, I couldn't resist." He licked his lips and stepped in close, the fire behind him casting his shadow over me.

"But you absolutely will resist tonight," I insisted, uneasy from his closeness.

He scowled. "It seems I have no choice but to obey you, although I wish you would reconsider. It would help us both if I were stronger."

The achingly desperate tone in his voice made me uneasy. "Explain."

"As I was saying." He swallowed, licking his lips. "Your blood is my ambrosia. I can hear it in your veins, smell it on your breath. I gave in to temptation that first night and I was hooked. An instant addict. That addiction made me vulnerable. I may have fallen in love with you a little that day."

"That's not love," I said.

The dark look he gave me left me sipping my scotch, thankful for the burn in my throat.

He sipped his too. "Of course, once your caretaker rescued you, I stayed away. I tried to forget the feel of you beneath me. I found other diversions."

"Like Calliope?"

"Yes.

"But then Tabetha came along."

"Fucking witch. One bite of her contaminated tart and I was her plaything, but the worst part was the entombment. Decimated under Tabetha's tree, I spent an inordinate amount of time thinking of you." He chuckled mockingly. "Two thousand years of memories and *you* are what my wasted mind couldn't forget. *You* were what I remembered when I couldn't control my own thoughts. A witch I could not have. A witch who didn't want me. I dreamt of you until…" He shook his head and laughed.

I gasped. "Until I fed you my blood."

He tapped the tip of his nose. "Yes. Imagine my surprise to see *you* hovering over me. I appreciate the gesture, but did you know what your blood would do to me?"

"Of course not."

"Neither did I. Not until Polina mentioned that you shouldn't have fed me. Later that night, I wanted to go after Bathory to finish her." He shook his head. "Instead, I rescued *you*."

"Uh… Thank you."

Julius scowled. "I did some research on the topic of interspecies blood sharing. As it turns out, you are a sorceress of the dead, and I am technically dead. *Your* blood in my veins is a toxin. It is heroin to my kind. I fear Polina is right, and it has made me your slave."

"It didn't have to. You knew about the addictive qualities of my blood before you rescued me in Salem. You must've known your blood could heal me or you wouldn't have offered it. Even if what you say is true and you didn't understand the bond or what your blood would do to me, you chose to take the third taste, anyway. Why did you lick the blood from my neck? Why save me from the goblin at all?"

He set his drink down and held out his hand to me. "Come. Let me show you."

I allowed him to help me from the plush chair and lead me around the bed to a desk near the bar. "You're not going to show me an ancient picture of a long-dead girlfriend who looks exactly like me, are you?"

He frowned. "No. Why would I do that?"

"No reason."

On top of the desk, a large calendar acted as a blotter. He paged back to the night in March when I'd saved him from Tabetha, more than three weeks ago. A red X marked the day. "That was the last time I fed on a live human's blood, besides the little I licked from your neck."

"That was the night I fed you at Tabetha's. That was weeks ago."

He released my hand and leaned over the desk, bracing himself. "In almost two thousand years, I have never lost my appetite for human blood. You have ruined me."

"I haven't *ruined* you."

"Every time I come close to a vein, all I see is you. All I feel is your pulse on my tongue. I licked the blood off your neck that night because I was starving, Grateful. I had no choice."

"It's not my fault. I didn't know."

He turned his face to look at me. "I'd hoped to feed you my blood. I'd hoped we could have some kind of arrangement. I see now that you don't want that. Only *my* side of this *mistake* can't be undone. Only *I* have to live with the consequences."

I saw it then, in his eyes. The suffering. The agony. He was bound to me. Hungry and wanting.

"You can't have made it this long without eating anything." I shook my head. "You'd be a skeleton."

"I can tolerate animals."

"There, see, not so bad." I patted his shoulder.

He gave me a look that would solder iron. "It's torture!" he snapped. "You've made the one pleasure of my infinite existence empty. Let me ask you, Grateful, would you enjoy eating cardboard for three meals a day for eternity?"

"I'm sorry, Julius, but none of this would have happened if you hadn't almost killed me that first night. A little self-control could have kept you out of this mess."

He jerked back like I'd burned him and backed away. "Do you think I don't rue the day I ever tasted your blood? Do you think I don't regret ever meeting you?" He pressed a hand into his chest and shook his head. "Don't mistake me for someone with no self-control, witch. You had my blood in your hand only moments ago."

Cold realization made my breath hitch. "You put your blood in my scotch!" I raised my hands to my mouth.

"Yes. Your first scotch. The one you did not drink."

I backed up, heart pounding, and sat on the bed. "I didn't drink it. I never drank your blood."

"No. You never drank my blood," he said cynically. "Thanks to me. Thanks to me having some control."

I stared at him, his twisted morality coming into perspective. "No. It was because I ordered you not to give me your blood without my permission."

He sighed. "Despite what you think of me, I legitimately care for you. I wouldn't have let you drink it."

"Bullshit."

"Please... please promise me you will try to find a way to break the bond. I'm helping you by sheltering you here—sheltering you from a goddess. That should be worth something."

So that was why he was helping me. It wasn't just the bond but the promise of removing it. I sensed Julius would do anything toward that end.

"Deal. I'll find a way to break the bond," I said. I needed his help, and I didn't want him bound to me. With a deep breath, I met his gaze and felt genuine pity for the vampire. I couldn't call what he felt for me love. I hadn't broken his heart as Polina suggested, but I had taken something from him, something valuable and permanent. And if I could, I was more than willing to give it back.

He turned away and strode to a door near the back of the room. "Now, I promised you something to wear." He disappeared inside what I presumed was a closet, and when he emerged again, I could hardly believe my eyes.

"Should I ask where you got that?"

"No. But to put your mind at ease, let's just say the original owner left it here in the twenties and as far as I know lived a long and fruitful life."

"You kept it all this time?"

"Could you throw something like this away?" He said with a half grin. "I may be a vampire, but I'm not a monster."

CHAPTER 11
Changes

When I descended the steps from Julius's room, I attracted more than my share of attention. This time it wasn't because I was a witch or the state of my pajamas; it was the dress. The gown Julius lent me was vintage, silver silk beaded with Swarovski crystals from the spaghetti straps that crisscrossed along my back to the ankle-length hem. The dress was old-Hollywood glamorous, with a high neckline in front, a nonexistent back, and a slit that hit mid-thigh. My only secret was Nightshade, secured carefully to my covered leg, and Tabetha's wand, tucked into the sheath beside her.

The matching shoes were a half-size too big, and I gripped the railing for fear of falling. As I descended, I searched the crowd for Rick. I found him at the bar between two female vampires who leaned in on either side, crowding his personal space with unjustified familiarity. Their mouths moved as if they were carrying on a lively conversation with my caretaker. I couldn't tell if Rick was participating because his back was to me.

The moment he sensed my presence, his shoulders rolled back and the muscles of his torso tensed. In a series of jerky and incremental movements, he twisted to look at me. The weight of his stare was a tangible thing, his gray gaze burning everywhere it touched. I stopped at the base of the stairs and simply breathed through the intensity of it. There was attraction in that look, for sure, but it was more than that. Rick's gaze held possession, longing, hunger.

He stood from the bar and strode toward me, to the disappointment of his female accompaniment, who flashed fang my direction before turning back toward their drinks. Tonight, there was no mistaking Rick for human. Red wine in hand, he navigated the crowd with the swagger of an animal, his muscles rolling and stretching as if his entire body was double-jointed. He stopped short of touching me, close enough that I could feel his body heat.

"You are enchanting," he whispered.

A hot blush warmed my neck and ears. I had to avert my eyes; his stare was too penetrating. "Thank you." My attention caught on his glass, and I wrapped my fingers around the stem. "Do you mind if I share a sip?"

He shook his head and retracted the glass. "It's blood. They serve a number of flavors here. They tell me this is from a Scandinavian woman. I have nothing to compare it to aside from yours. It doesn't come close, but it suited my needs." All levity drained from his face, and he abandoned the blood on a nearby table.

I placed a hand on his cheek and turned his face toward me. "Don't be ashamed for eating when you're hungry. I just wish you had told me. I'd prefer you get the blood from me."

"I don't like to hurt you."

"When you fed me yesterday, did it hurt you?"

"No. In fact it was... pleasurable." He lowered his chin and peered at me through long, dark lashes.

I smiled, rubbing my thumb along his cheek. "It's the same for me."

A soft inhale parted his lips. "Would you dance with me?" he asked.

By way of response, I took his hand and led him to the dance floor. The band was playing a slow blues number, the cries of the trumpet breaking through the candlelight. I guided Rick's hands to my waist and wrapped my arms around his neck.

"I suppose you didn't dance like this in the seventeenth century," I said.

His grip tightened and he pulled me closer, flat against his charcoal gray T-shirt. We swayed to the music, and I melted into his embrace. His lips grazed the top of my ear as he said, "I am beginning to see the advantages of no longer living in the seventeenth century, Isabella."

"Grateful," I corrected, pulling back a little. "My name is Grateful, Rick."

He searched my face. "Of course, now, but you were her. You were her once."

I frowned. "Once. A long time ago, a part of me existed that was Isabella, but I'm different than her. I'm my own person with my own life and my own history."

He stiffened. "Yesterday, when you were in my arms, I felt her, my Isabella, the woman I loved. She was you."

I stopped dancing. "An echo, maybe. Rick, you can't think of me as Isabella. It's true we share an immortal soul and a source of power that is eternal, but my body, my memories, and my experiences are my own. I'm an entirely different person."

His jaw tightened with his grip, and he pulled me closer again. "I am sorry, Grateful. I did not mean to be presumptuous. The feelings I have toward you are confusing to me. Ancient. Intense."

"Our relationship has always been… physical." I licked my lips. "It's nothing to be ashamed of. You told me it happens every time."

"Every time?"

"Every time I die and come back. You find me, every time, and we fall in love again."

"Sounds simple. Almost inevitable." His eyes shifted to the floor and the corners of his mouth curled under.

With a little shake, I tried to refocus his attention on me. "Affairs of the heart are never simple, and I'm not naïve enough to believe that anything is inevitable. You have a choice. You don't have to…" My voice cracked, but

I forced myself to finish. "…love me. You don't have to love me."

The music stopped. We weren't dancing anyway. The band started packing up their instruments and small groups of vampires quietly disappeared around the corner to the tunnels. The crowd parted like water around us, our bodies motionless rocks in a sea of activity.

I looked away from Rick only when a mass of black feathers almost barreled into my head.

"Poe!" He landed on my shoulder and rubbed his birdy body against my ear.

"Thank the goddess," Poe said. "I looked everywhere."

"I knew you'd find me eventually. If we'd waited, I'd be dead."

Gary appeared, looking haggard and barely conscious. He rolled a small suitcase toward me, the worn carry-on my father gave me in high school, and shoved the handle into my hand. "Julius told me to tell you to take the bed. He prefers one of the guest coffins."

"Where'd you get this?" I asked, taking it from him.

"Sent a human back to your place." With a small, sarcastic salute, Gary disappeared in the direction of the tunnels.

I glanced at Rick, suddenly feeling exhausted. He motioned toward the stairs. "After you, *Grateful*."

* * * * *

As I led Rick to Julius's room, I felt like a predator. I was exhausted and needed rest above all things, but in the back of my mind, all I could think about was getting him between those red silk sheets. He wasn't ready for this level of seduction. Not emotionally or mentally. But I couldn't help myself. I was starving.

I parked my suitcase next to the door and turned the lock. With eyes on him, I crossed to the side of the bed closest to the fireplace and kicked off my shoes. "Will you join me tonight?" I asked, biting my lip. I hooked one hand around the bedpost and leaned out, swaying slightly. "Watch over me while I sleep?"

He swallowed and gave a curt nod. With careful steps, he approached.

I stopped swinging and stood up straight, letting the smile drain from my face. Then I hooked my fingers under the straps of the silver dress and slid them from my shoulders. The fabric crumpled to the floor, leaving me bared in the light of the fire.

Rick stopped short. "You've been scarred."

I looked down at myself. The place between my breasts where Hecate had burned me now bore a jagged scab.

"Does this bother you?" I asked.

For a moment, he simply stared, impassive.

"I'm sorry," I said, bending to retrieve my dress. "I've pushed you too far."

In a flash, strong arms swooped me up by the waist and crushed me against his chest. My legs wrapped easily, naturally, over his hips, and he supported me under my thighs.

"I'll tell you when you've gone to far. As you said, our relationship has always been physical," he whispered into my lips. His mouth crashed into mine.

Frantically, I tugged at the hem of his T-shirt. He tipped me onto the bed, my back bouncing on the red velvet, before stripping the gray cotton over his head. I sat up and went to work on his fly. I was hungry, starving for his touch in more ways than one. That metaphysical connection we shared awakened, his need for me all animal attraction and raw heat. I worked my hand into his pants, cradling and stroking. His breath came in ragged pants, and he froze, hinging at the hips.

"What's wrong?" I asked.

"Forgive me. I am losing myself."

I took his hand and placed it over my heart. "Do you remember any of this? Sex, I mean."

He shook his head and lowered his eyes. "It is clear my body remembers, but I have never done this before."

I guided his hand until it cupped my breast. "It's normal to feel like you're losing control."

His thumb stroked my nipple and he relaxed slightly.

"Take your time." I slowed my fondling and brushed his lips with my own.

He kissed me back, caressing my breast and melding his mouth with mine.

"Oh!" I said, pulling away a little. I reached up and dabbed my bleeding lip. Rick had partially shifted and clipped my lip with his eyetooth.

He looked at me with widened black eyes.

"It's okay," I cooed, continuing to stroke him. "Remember how it was in your bedroom? Your beast comes to the surface when you have strong emotions."

A violent shiver coursed the length of his back. "I can't s-stop it."

"Oh!" The skin of his chest and arms bubbled ominously. I removed my hand from his pants. Rick hadn't shifted since he lost his memory. "This isn't the most ideal venue for your first time shifting, but I think it's important you let it happen," I said to him. Once he was over this hurdle, I was sure his beast would be easier to control. He needed to be able to defend himself. "Don't try to stop it. Let it go."

I scooted off the bed and moved toward the fire to give him more space. He backed away, his body convulsing. Bones snapped and organs shifted beneath his bubbling skin. He released a wretched scream.

"What's wrong? What's happening?" Shifting didn't usually hurt Rick. In fact, he'd told me before that it was painless.

"It hurts. Oh God, help me!"

I closed my eyes and opened our metaphysical connection. He'd paused mid-shift and was indeed in excruciating pain. "Don't block it, Rick," I said. Why was he stuck? This had never happened. I tugged on that string that bound us together, coaxing his beast out with my magic.

He screamed again, and I pulled harder. His black eyes met mine as the bones of his back elongated into a tail and claws sprouted from his bent knuckles. He couldn't speak anymore but down our connection, he was begging for help.

"Let it go," I cried. "You're only making it worse trying to stop it." I coaxed and pulled until I was sweating from the effort.

With one last tear of flesh, the man who was Rick was gone and the dragon-like creature I called *the beast* filled the space in the large room. Two iridescent leather wings unfolded from his back. Rick's beast whimpered and lowered his head, lifting one foot, then another.

I reached out to stroke him behind the ear.

Wild-eyed, the beast retreated from my hand, then roared loud and long enough to blow back my hair. "What's wrong, big guy?" I asked sweetly.

The beast rolled one giant black eye toward me until I could see my reflection in it. Thumping down to the floor, it whimpered again. This time when I reached out, it closed its eyes and allowed me to scratch and massage its neck.

"I'm not sure why that was so painful. It's usually not that bad," I whispered. I stroked his neck until the beast's eyes grew heavy and his breath even. "Okay, Rick, time to change back. Try to relax."

The beast jerked away again, bumping against the bookshelves in panic. Several heavy volumes rained down on his scaly hide. I reached down our metaphysical connection and pushed the beast away, calling Rick's form forth.

His scales shifted and ruptured. The beast's wings folded into its back and its claws retracted into flesh. A process Rick used to accomplish in seconds took several painful minutes and more than a little help from me. Finally, Rick unfolded, naked and shaking. He was ghostly pale and sweat made his skin glisten in the firelight. He groaned and tumbled onto the bed.

"Let me help you," I said, moving to his side.

"Don't touch me." He flinched away, tucking himself under the blanket. "I… I am sorry. Everything hurts. I cannot bear it."

"It will get easier, Rick. Every time you shift, the process will go faster and hurt less." At least I thought it would. That's how it had been before.

He held up one hand and curled into a ball on his side.

I crawled in beside him, although the terribly large bed meant we both had plenty of room. Hand reaching for him over the mattress, I paused and squashed my desire to comfort him with physical touch. Staring at his back across the long stretch of mattress, I whispered, "Rick, are you okay? Do you need blood?"

"The answer to both of those questions is no," he said. "Go to sleep, Grateful. You need rest, and I cannot speak to you right now."

I licked my lips and coiled within myself like a tight spring. "Okay." I stared at his back until sleep finally overcame me.

CHAPTER 12
You again

The clink of dish against dish woke me. I blinked to clear my sleepy vision and found Julius sitting with a newspaper in one of the red chairs near the fireplace. The fire had gained several new logs and the blaze produced a homey atmosphere at odds with its supernatural occupant. He'd turned the massive piece of furniture slightly, I assumed so he could watch me sleep. Creepy. The clinking I'd heard must have been his teacup hitting the saucer. The hot liquid still sloshed against the rim. A large plate of scones rested on a small table next to him.

"You again." I groaned.

"Good morning to you too." He scowled in my general direction.

"What are you doing in here? I thought I locked the door."

"And I have the key. It is my safe house." He refolded the paper and raised an eyebrow. "Breakfast?"

I looked over my shoulder, but the bed was empty. "Where's Rick?"

"He's downstairs partaking in a flight of blood. Seems you wore him out last night." Julius's eyes raked over my body.

That's when I remembered I was naked. I snatched the velvet comforter from my waist and dragged it up to my neck.

"Don't cover up on my account. I was quite enjoying the view." With a sigh, he tucked the paper beside him in the chair and raised his cup. A muscle in his jaw twitched. "Why didn't you tell me about the mark?"

"What mark?" I looked down at myself. "Oh, that. It's a scar from where Hecate attacked me. Red lightning straight to the heart."

"It's not a scar. It's ancient Greek."

I stared at my chest under the blanket, at the sharp edges and geometric shapes carved into my skin. "No... What?"

"It is ancient Greek. Your mother left you a message in your skin."

"What does it say?"

He struck me with an intense stare. "It says, *I give permission*. You've been marked, Grateful."

"Fuck me!"

"Is that an invitation?"

I scowled and sat up, wrapping the blanket around me and allowing the sheet to slip from my skin. I managed well enough to keep all the important parts covered, but when he thought I wasn't looking, Julius's eyes shifted to the place where the edges of the blanket met. I took a seat opposite him and poured myself a cup of tea.

"I need to tell Rick. Every supernatural baddie in the ward is going to have a taste for my blood."

"I recommend you keep the mark covered and remain as under the radar as possible."

"But what then? I can't hide forever."

"If you can't hide, then you must fight."

I peeked over my cup at the vampire, but there was no hint of levity or condescension in his eyes, only pity.

"I should get dressed and find Rick." I set down the tea and stood, searching the room for my bag.

"He doesn't look well. What happened last night?"

"He shifted for the first time since he lost his memory."

Julius lifted his teacup and took a contemplative sip. "Then my suspicions were correct. The caretaker's abilities have been compromised, as well as his memories. He is not 'fine' as you so firmly insisted."

The bag Gary had provided me was hastily packed. I wondered briefly which human companion he'd sent back to the house. Instead of answering Julius, I ducked into the bathroom and changed into jeans and a long sleeved

T-shirt. When I emerged minutes later, the vampire looked at me expectantly.

I sank into the chair across from him and broke off a corner of a scone. "What do you want from me? An apology?"

"An apology from you would be as rare as a snowball in July. I'd settle for an admission of the truth."

I popped the pastry into my mouth. Buttery. Rich. Delicious. "Fine. Rick's not himself… yet."

Julius leaned forward and tapped the tips of his fingers together between his knees. "If we are going to work together, you must be honest with me. I have risked my life and my coven helping you."

"He can't do magic, okay? Like, none. Not even caretaker magic. When he shifted last night, it was painful to watch. I've never seen him shift so slowly or suffer so much. I had to use our connection to help things along."

Julius grimaced.

"What? I couldn't leave him half-shifted like that. It was torture."

The vampire crossed one leg over the other and leaned back into the plush chair. "If I understand correctly, Tabetha's persigranate poisoning was meant to turn him into a vegetable. You intercepted the spell but not before damage was done. The last thing Rick remembers was seeing you burn. He's lost everything between then and now."

"Exactly. The faster we can help him accept what he is and relearn what he's lost, the better."

"What if it isn't just about relearning?" he said, returning his cup to the table and leaning toward me. "What if something was supposed to happen in 1698 after you burned? What if the caretaker spell was undone or never fully completed?"

I dropped the scone I was holding. It landed in my lap and dusted me with crumbs. For a long time, all I could do was stare at Julius. How could this vamp see what I had missed all these weeks? Rick hadn't just forgotten who he was and what he could do. He was a puzzle with a missing piece.

I stood. The pastry fell to the floor, scattering crumbs everywhere.

"Grateful, this is an old building. You'll attract rats." He charged across the room to the door and yelled something down the hall. I wasn't listening. I was pacing.

"In 1698, after I burned to death, Rick was able to build and enchant the fence around Monk's Hill Cemetery. That means, his full power came to him almost immediately," I said. What was the catalyst between my burning and his coming to power? What tidbit of history had been unraveled by Tabetha's mischief?

A female vamp in a maid's uniform rushed past me with a dustpan and began cleaning up the mess.

"I need my grimoire," I said to Julius.

"Out of the question. Your house is surrounded. The goblins will make Swiss cheese of you before you reach it."

"Gary got someone in."

Julius shook his head. "Gary compelled a human to go in on his behalf, at dawn while the goblins were still distracted with your escape."

I squinted at him. "Which human did Gary compel?"

"Your friend Logan."

"What? Why?"

"Valentine's. It's nearby and accessible. Gary only had a few moments before dawn."

"Damn it, Julius. I promised myself I'd keep Logan out of this mess. He's been through enough with Tabetha. You shouldn't have used him like that!"

The vampire scowled and paced toward me, wrapping his icy fingers around the bare skin of my shoulders. "You, witch, are in need of a reality check. A goddess wants you dead. One misstep, one wrong move, and all is lost. All you have going for you is a faulty caretaker, a mangy familiar, and a vampire, weak from drinking animal blood. Now, I am truly sorry that your high principles were affronted by our use of your friend, but if you'd like to live another day, I suggest you quickly build a bridge and get over it."

"Mangy? Speak for yourself, corpse breath." Poe swooped through the door left open by the maid and landed on the back of my recently vacated chair.

"Poe, where have you been?" I asked.

"Out gathering reinforcements," he said, nodding toward the door.

Polina appeared in the doorway with Hildegard, her snowy white barn owl, on her shoulder. She placed her fists on the hips of her leather pants. "Poe tells us there's been trouble."

CHAPTER 13
A Team of My Own

After explaining about the second goblin attack, Julius's interpretation of my scar, and Rick's painful shifting experience, I waited impatiently for Polina's reaction. She paced the large room, her frown becoming incrementally more pronounced with every step. The intensity of her movement caused Hildegard to leave her shoulder and perch next to Poe on the canopy of the bed.

"If I had any sense, I'd kill you right now and be done with this," she said.

"Excuse me?" I could tell she wasn't serious, but I didn't like where this conversation was headed.

"I like you, Grateful. You're one of my only friends. But you must realize a quick death would be the compassionate end for you. The goddess has a price on your head. Every supernatural being is going to want you dead, if not to improve their position, then to gain favor with the goddess."

"Yeah, because that worked out so well for me when I had permission to kill Tabetha."

"You know that and I know that, but there are plenty of witches who will lick their chops at the thought of gaining not one but two elements with your death. And if the criminal supernaturals gets wind of this? They'll want you dead to be free of your judgment. I highly doubt the goblins will be the only ones aiming for your head."

"Let's just say I don't want to march quietly into that good night. What are my other options?"

Polina crossed her arms over her chest. "Exile? A good cloaking spell might keep you safe for a time."

The fire crackled as I contemplated where I'd go and how I'd say goodbye to the ones I loved.

"You can't seriously be considering this," Julius said. We both turned to see him shaking his head. "It's inconceivable. A woman like Grateful Knight does not run or hide."

"Really? Because I thought the hiding sounded like a good option."

He gripped the back of the red chair and smirked. "No, no, no. The answer, dear witches, is right in front of you. Hecate handed it to you on a silver platter."

"Out with it," I said.

"The only way to appease her is to do the very thing she thinks you wouldn't dare to do—unite the elements." He pointed one elegant finger in my direction. "You kill an earth, metal, and water witch and you'll have enough power to not only break the bond between us as you promised, but to tell Mummy to take a hike."

A conspicuous silence fell across the room. My gaze darted to Polina. She'd drawn her wand and didn't look happy. I couldn't blame her. Julius had just suggested I kill her, and she understood my bond with Julius meant every vampire in this safe house was mine to command.

Poe broke the tension with a long low whistle, and I found my voice.

"I'm not killing anyone." I held up one hand toward my half-sister. "Polina, I would never hurt you." I met her gaze and lowered my chin. "You know I would never hurt you, right, Polina?"

She hesitated for a moment. "I believe you, Grateful, but Tabetha started out as benevolent as you. Power changes people. It corrupts. I swear to the goddess if I get one hint you are changing or becoming like Tabetha, I will use Mother's permission and kill you." She pointed her wand at me.

Julius appeared between us in a flash, hissing and flashing his fangs.

"Relax, Julius," I said. "Polina needs to take care of herself. I don't blame her. And frankly, I'd rather die than end up like Tabetha."

Polina lowered her wand. "For now, I trust you, and I have no plans to kill you despite the permission."

"Good, because I have a plan." My eyes darted between Poe, Julius, and Polina. "We do as Julius suggests and combine the elements—"

"I thought you just said—"

I shook my head. "Not by killing. By collaboration. We convince other witches to lend me their powers, just temporarily. Once I unite the elements, I'll set things right and give them all back."

She narrowed her eyes at me. "Are you insane? No witch is going to trust you with her power because you *promise* you'll give it back." She snorted. "It's laughable."

"I hold air and wood. Rick holds earth. If you agree to help me, I have metal. All we need is a water witch to cooperate. Just one. We should be able to convince one witch to help us."

"You think you can convince a water witch you've never met to join up and loan her power to you for no other reason than generosity?" Polina asked.

"Exactly."

"That may be optimism at its finest," Julius murmured. "Killing would be easier. And your presumption about Rick is positively ludicrous. Have you forgotten that he has no magic?"

"It's in him, somewhere. He just doesn't remember. If he had it before, there must be a way for him to have it again." I flashed a warning look at Julius. Polina didn't need to hear about Rick's shortcomings now, not when I was trying to convince her to join my cause.

Polina traced her lips with her fingers. "Tabetha's persigranate shouldn't have affected his elemental power. Even if he doesn't know how to use it, we should be able to leverage his magic."

I nodded my agreement. "And, worst-case scenario, if we can't, we can find and convince an earth witch too." I chewed my lip. One witch was a long shot. Two would be winning the lottery.

Poe rolled his eyes. "Why not? I'm sure witches will be lining up to loan you their powers in order to make you invincible."

"Poe is right. No witch is going to help you do this, Grateful, unless you force her. It's too risky," Polina said.

"What about you?" I asked, looking her in the eye. "Let's get this out on the table. Will you help me, Polina?"

She grimaced and took a deep breath. "I will, but…"

"If I've convinced you, I can convince someone else."

"I have to help you. I was standing behind you in Hecate's garden. What makes you think I won't be the next on her hit list? I have to help you, but other witches won't. Even if they feel for you, they'll want to distance themselves."

"Maybe. Maybe not. We won't know until we try."

Poe sighed. "It could work, if you can find willing witches to participate, don't allow them to kill you first, and are able to complete the spell to unite the elements before the goddess or her hired thugs strike you down."

Damn, this was shaping up to be one hell of a tall order. I spread my hands. "Does anyone have a better idea?"

Poe exchanged glances with Polina and Julius.

"I don't," Polina said. "But even *you* must realize this is risky. If I were you, I'd have some hard conversations with the important people in my life."

"You mean Rick."

"He's the one who will have to help bring you back if you get killed enacting this plan."

I bit my lip. She was right. At a minimum, I needed to prepare Rick for my demise and reincarnation.

"My vampires can help," Julius said. "Depending on the witch, I might even be able to compel her cooperation."

"Thank you."

"I'm not being generous. In exchange for my help, I expect you to break this bond you hold over me as soon as you are powerful enough to do so."

"Of course. I promised you I would. Are you sure you want to help me? It could mean your eternal life."

He looked at me and without a hint of smile said, "Woman, as long as I'm bound to you, I'm dead anyway."

Hildegard stretched and flapped her snowy wings. Polina's magical familiar couldn't speak human English like Poe, but her witch understood her as if she could.

"Hildegard offers her support. She says she'll persuade the witch's familiar, should she have one, to help our cause," Polina said.

"How about you, Poe? Are you in?"

Poe rolled his eyes. "Of course I am. Your existence is my existence."

Julius bowed slightly at the waist. "I am at your service."

Polina nodded solemnly. "I'm in."

"We can do this! And when it's all over, Hecate will leave me alone because she'll know I don't want to be a goddess."

There was a light knock on the door. Julius glanced at me, then flashed across the room to open it. The maid who'd cleaned up the scone stood with her hands folded in front of her hips.

"I am sorry to disturb you, but there is a problem with a patron downstairs, Master Julius."

"A problem?" Julius asked, turning his ear to the hall.

"The man your guest brought with her"—she gestured toward me—"has started a brawl."

I pushed past Julius and rushed into the hall. "Oh no. Rick!"

CHAPTER 14
Fight! Fight! Fight!

I sprinted into the bar just in time to see Rick's fist connect with Gary's face. Vampires are tough, but caretakers are tougher. A caretaker's purpose is to balance the darkness in the world. He's made to be as hard and fast as a vampire, as strong as a shifter, as enduring as a poltergeist. Even in his current state of disconnectedness, Rick was a formidable force.

Gary hit the floor and slid across the waxed wood planks into the wall, parting the crowd of vampire patrons who smiled and swirled their drinks at the impromptu entertainment. At super speed, Gary bounced to his toes and tackled Rick into the bar. The crowd cheered. More annoyed than injured, my caretaker brought an elbow down on Gary's head, eliciting a yelp from the vamp and a groan from the audience.

"Stop. Stop!" I yelled, drawing Nightshade.

My blade glowed like a lightsaber and the bar plunged into silence. The band stopped playing. The bartender stopped serving drinks. A squirrelly vamp perched on a barstool dropped his drink and glass shattered near his feet. He didn't stoop to pick it up. Every eye locked on Nightshade.

I approached Rick, who still had Gary's neck in a chokehold.

"What is going on here?" I asked.

Rick's mouth twisted in disgust. "This... this... creature said he was previously intimate with you."

"I just mentioned we used to live together, Grateful," Gary whined.

I rolled my eyes. "Why would you do that, Gary? Does this seem like the time or the place?" I pulled Gary out of Rick's grip by the collar and pushed him away.

"You can't be suggesting..." Rick looked at Gary in disgust.

"I was trying to commiserate with the guy," Gary pleaded with me, spreading his hands. "He's down here drinking all night, blubbering on about how confusing you are. Now I'm the bad guy for agreeing with him?" Gary swatted the air between us. "Forgive me for caring."

Rick's nostrils flared. "You are a liar. This woman would never touch you." He swayed on his feet.

I caught him by the chest. "Are you drunk?" I didn't know Rick could get drunk. In as long as I'd known him, I'd never seen him like this.

"He's been drinking rum-laced blood all night. Anything would get drunk on that," Gary said. "Even a caretaker."

"Hmm." I slipped my arm around Rick's waist. "Come upstairs with me and we'll sort this all out." He nodded, and we ambled toward the stairs. Out of the corner of my eye, I caught Gary following. "Not you, Gary." The vampire threw up his hands and sat down at the nearest table.

Julius, who had followed me into the bar, crossed the room to talk with the bartender, frowning slightly at my hold on Rick.

I manipulated him up the stairs, into Julius's room, and plunked him down next to the fire. Polina, Poe, and Hildegard slipped out the door without saying a word.

"How do you know that vampire?" Rick slurred. I could smell the rum on his breath. Who knew rum-laced blood was even a thing?

Taking the chair across from him, I sighed heavily. "I'm tempted to lie to you right now, but I don't think that's a good way to start or continue a relationship."

"Lie to me about what?" His head circled and his eyelids fluttered. He propped himself on his knees.

"Gary wasn't always a vampire. He used to be human, and before I met you, he used to be my boyfriend."

Rick's lazy eyes widened and he slouched back in his chair looking thoroughly dejected.

"I'm sorry, Rick. It's not something I'm proud of. The thing is, I didn't know."

He shook his head. "You didn't know? You didn't know you were dating Gary?"

"No. Not that. I didn't know there would be a you. If I'd known all I'd have to do is wait and my soulmate would come to me, I would have waited."

He grunted.

"No, really. Someone can tell you the ocean is big, but until you stand on its shores, you can never fully appreciate how completely humbled you become in its presence. People told me about love, Rick. I thought I could create it if I worked hard enough, but I didn't know. You can't create what we have, not even with magic. It just is, and it's humbling and it's larger than life."

He leaned forward and placed a hand on my cheek. His gray eyes connected with mine, and I could see the love he had for me. Wasn't that what this was all about with Gary? If he didn't have feelings for me, he wouldn't be jealous. His lips parted and my heart trembled.

"I remember having that," Rick said.

I grinned like a kid at Christmas.

"With Isabella."

My smile faded along with the swell of hope in my bosom.

"Part of her is in you. I feel it. Even now, sitting across from you, I sense her under the surface. I don't remember the rest. I wish I did. It would make this easier."

"I know."

"I believe you, about our history, but Grateful, last night…"

"We moved too fast."

"No, not that," he said, surprising me. "What happened to me, when I changed, it was excruciating. It felt wrong, forced. It was torture." He stared at his hands, a slight tremor forming in the fingers. "I'm afraid of it happening again. I want to be what you need me to be, but I can't do that again." He shook his head, then shifted away from me, eyes drifting to the fire.

A lump formed in my throat. It was devastating to see him like this, like the pain of shifting had broken him, and to know I was responsible. I cleared my throat. "I have a theory about what happened." Actually, it was Julius's theory, but given the night Rick was having, I kept that nugget of info to myself. "I think Tabetha's spell wiped out more than your memory. I think you lost a piece of your power. Maybe a piece of our connection. I'm going to find out what's missing and give it back to you."

"And then what?"

"And then it shouldn't hurt anymore when you shift."

He scrubbed his face with his palms. "Why is this so important to you?" he muttered under his breath.

I crossed to him and placed my hand on his shoulder. Eventually, he lifted his face to mine. "It's only important to me because I want you to be able to protect yourself. You're immortal, but that doesn't mean you can't be captured, tortured, even torn apart. If something happens to me…"

His eyelids drooped and his head wavered. He was falling asleep sitting up.

"You're tired," I said.

He opened his eyes a crack. "I suppose I am. Is this a common problem with too much drink?"

"Very common. Come on." I helped him from the chair to the bed and tucked him between the sheets. On a whim, I leaned over and kissed him on the forehead. "I love you, Rick," I whispered. "No matter what. Whether or not you can shift."

He didn't open his eyes.

* * * * *

Back downstairs, I pulled up a chair across from Polina, who sat alone in a dark corner with a glass of something pale yellow and bubbly. A heavyset black vampire onstage sang "I Put a Spell on You" by Nina Simone. Couples swayed on the dance floor, the night's earlier fight forgotten for more romantic pursuits.

"Mind if I join you?" I asked.

She motioned her red head toward the chair next to her. "Julius said he needed to take care of some business before we embarked on our quest to find a water witch."

"Did you ask what kind of business?"

She shook her head and lifted her glass. "Better if I don't know. I've got a real problem trusting that guy,

Grateful. I understand involving him is necessary, if we are to have any hope of keeping you alive, but"—she shivered—"he gives me the creeps." Raising her glass, she took a deep swig.

"What are you drinking?" I asked.

"Champagne. 1926 Dom Perignon. The vampires don't like it. Charged me six bucks." She laughed.

"That champagne is priceless."

"I know!"

I raised my hand to call over the brunette waitress with the fangy overbite. "I'll have what she's having."

"You didn't come down here to drink. What happened to your caretaker?"

"Asleep. Too much laced blood."

"Probably a good idea he gets his rest. We need him at his best."

"That's what I came down here to talk to you about. I need your help."

"Helping you unite the elements isn't enough? You need something else?"

The waitress arrived with my drink, and I took a long swig. "I need to do a spell to find out what happened to Rick after I died in 1698. Julius thinks he didn't just forget me. He thinks part of my caretaker spell was corrupted by Tabetha's magic."

"Do you think he's right?"

"I'm starting to. When I tried to use my magic mirror with him—the one you made for me—it felt like something was missing. And then last night, when he shifted, it was excruciating for him, almost like he didn't have enough magic to complete the transition. I had to use my power to help him. There's something going on. This can't all be due to his memory loss."

"Julius should send someone to get your grimoire. You could ask it to show you the day you executed the spell."

"I thought of that. The problem is that my grimoire can only show me my own experiences. I think what Rick lost happened after I was dead."

"That would be a very unusual spell. It's more likely you completed the spell before you died, and then Rick triggered the magic posthumously. You might be able to see that."

"But I won't know what I'm missing because I can't see what I can't see."

"True."

I finished my champagne and decided to go for broke. "I was wondering if you could use your crystal ball to show me what happened to Rick after I died." I scraped my teeth over my lower lip. I didn't even know if it was possible, but since the mirror Polina made me could see into the future, I thought it might be possible for her to see into the past.

"Crystal ball won't work. It's round, you know, like a planet. It's more of a logistical tool. You want to travel to another dimension, the ball is your tool." She pointed at me.

"I understand. I'll find a way to get to my grimoire and hope for the best."

"I didn't say I couldn't do it, just that I wouldn't use my crystal ball. A mirror is a much better tool for your purpose."

"Do you have one with you?"

"A small one. Not big enough to see what you want, but I can make one."

"I don't understand."

"I'll show you. Come on, we'd better do this before Julius gets back."

"Why?"

"He kills my vibe."

"Fair enough. Where should we start?"

CHAPTER 15
Old Demons

Polina found the items she needed behind the bar. The bartender wasn't happy to have her rummaging in his territory, but once I reminded him I was Julius's special guest, he didn't deny us. "He'll be very angry if you're the reason we can't complete our duties," I said. All hail the vampire bond. If I had to be associated with a vampire, I might as well partake of the benefits.

We ended up in a guest room that was barely larger than a closet and contained a single, thankfully empty, guest coffin. Spooky, but private.

"Candles, please," she said. We sat across from each other, a deep silver tray between us, large enough to sport a Thanksgiving turkey. The candles themselves were already set up around the room. What she wanted was for me to light them.

"Got it." I took a deep breath and blew. The wicks ignited, one after the other, until the entire room was bathed in candlelight.

"Good. Now I need your ring."

"My engagement ring?" The bed of blue stones I wore on my finger was my most cherished possession. Rick had given me the ring the first time we were married and every time after that. Multiple lifetimes. Multiple weddings. I couldn't fathom the idea of losing it. "You won't, like, melt it down or anything, will you?"

"I won't do anything that can't be undone."

"Hmm." For some reason, that didn't make me feel any better. Reluctantly, I offed the ring and handed it to her. She tossed it into the pan where it rolled and clanked.

"I hope this works," I muttered.

"No guarantees. I've never done this, but in theory it's a simple spell."

"In theory," I mumbled, reaching for my ring.

She grasped my hand out of the air and leaned over the tray. "*Amani novato morae…*" she began to chant.

I didn't understand the spell, but I opened up and allowed the magic in. Our power swirled, weighing down the air. The ring rattled in the pan. In the tempest of magic, the candles flickered, causing shadows to dance across the silver. Polina's chanting had a meditative quality, and my mind blanked until I simply existed. My consciousness was a boat, bobbing on a sea of words and power. I'm not sure how long she chanted. Time became meaningless, and maybe that was the point.

The silver tray melted, flowing like mercury to thread through and around my ring, stretching and smoothing over until the reflection filled the room with light. And then we were there.

"Burn her! Kill the witch!" a woman in black wool and a white starched collar yelled.

We stood on the edge of an angry crowd. At the center, a beautiful woman with a long dark braid, brown skin, and full red lips struggled against the push and pull of angry hands. Isabella. This was my first incarnation. The townspeople, invoking the demonic spell from *The Book of Flesh and Bone*, dragged her away from us, up the hill to the church grounds.

I'd experienced this memory once, using my grimoire. Only then, I'd been inside my body looking out. It was worse watching it from this perspective, helpless to change anything. More horrific to be among the crowd. The hatred among them was toxic. It made me want to cover my ears. And they were thin, skeletal, starving. Tortured souls owned by the evil on their lips.

"Stop!" I yelled.

"They can't hear you," Polina said. "We are just observers here."

They forced her against the stake and used a braided cord to bind her. How easy it would have been for her to hover off that stake, had it not been for the spell holding her to her human form. Men pushed through the crowd to pile wood around her feet. I had to look away.

When I did, I saw Rick. At the back of the crowd, he paced, his hands balled into fists, his face lined with tears. There was nothing he could do. He didn't look any younger than the Rick I knew, only more innocent; the shine in his eyes and the way his full lips parted suggested a younger soul. It was the look of panic and helplessness on his face that broke my heart. He was human, utterly vulnerable, and completely broken.

The crowd parted and Reverend Monk emerged.

"Monk," Isabella sneered.

Reverend Monk was a man of small stature and the book he carried dwarfed him. I recognized the tome right away, *The Book of Flesh and Bone*. The pages were made of flayed human skin, the cover layered with the same. The ink contained human blood, and the inlaid design on the spine was not pearl but human teeth. According to legend, it was written by the Devil. I wasn't sure I believed in a devil, per se, but if there *was* a source of all evil and darkness, it certainly dwelled in that book.

"Finally, justice," Monk said.

"Justice? You call this justice? Burning an innocent woman without so much as a trial?" Isabella spat.

"Innocent?" Monk laughed. "The fire will prove your innocence."

"If I burn, I'm innocent, and if I don't, I'm a witch? That is my trial?"

Monk turned away, and one of the men approached, torch in hand. Isabella panted with fear, eyeing the book in Monk's hands. As the flames caught and licked up her body, I had to look away again. I couldn't force myself to watch. The screams were awful, worse when I smelled the burning flesh that used to be mine.

"Don't turn away, Grateful," Polina said. "This is the important part."

I turned back just as Isabella's left hand, charred and blackened, rose to waist level. Light shot from her fingers straight into Rick as her final words bubbled from her dying lips. *"Caretaker of the light, always."*

Rick's body seized, flopping to the ground and contorting in pain. The crowd turned in confusion.

"What's happening?" a woman cried.

"He is possessed by a demon," an elderly man chimed in. "The witch's lover. Burn him."

It was not Rick's seizure they should've feared. At that moment, an earthquake shook the crowd. Monk's parishioners screamed and gripped each other, cursing Rick for causing the violent quake. Darkness came on the wind. Thunder. Lightning. The earth split. Hellfire erupted from below. A woman in a full black skirt fell screaming into an open chasm. Reverend Monk burst into flames, dropping the cursed book, and one by one, the entire crowd met their end in fire and brimstone. The ground shifted, rolling their bodies into unmarked graves before closing around them. When the shaking stopped, the entire populace was buried.

All but Rick, who trembled at the base of Monk's Hill.

The wind picked up, and a giant saber-toothed cat with a forked tail burst from the forest. It scooped up *The Book of Flesh and Bone* in its teeth. Looking right through me, it returned the way it had come.

"What type of creature was that?" Polina asked.

"Nekomata," I answered, desperately wishing I could kill the beast before it got away. "Migrant shifters who collect magical objects. He'll bury that fucker in the empty plot behind us, in what will become the foundation of my house. Caused me a world of pain last year."

Polina squeezed my hand. "There's nothing you can do."

I scowled as the beast's backside disappeared into the forest, then turned my attention back on Rick. "This is it," I said. "Something should happen now that completes the transformation and gives Rick his magic."

Rick was unconscious, twitching from Isabella's spell. Watching him like this was difficult, curled like a bug in the dirt, the fires of hell burning in places on the hill, and the charred remains of Isabella looking over all of it. Aside from the occasional rustle of wind through overgrown grass, all was quiet.

All at once, the gray sky parted and a column of light descended, burning like a beacon and connecting the heavens and the earth near Rick's feet. The heat and power coming off the light blew my hair back and warmed my face.

"Do you feel that? That's not supposed to happen. We're not really here," Polina whispered. "What the fuck is that thing?"

The column of light took shape, gathering into a bright silhouette. The creature was humanoid, with flowing rays of light that trailed behind it like I'd never seen before—almost like wings.

"An angel?" I asked Polina, but she was struck dumb by the vision. Tears flowed down her cheeks. I was crying too, overwhelmed by the warmth, love, and light. I thought it must be an angel, but in fact, I had no name for what I was seeing. Humanoid, yes, but entirely made of light. The being placed what amounted to hands on either side of my caretaker's face.

Rick opened his eyes. His lips parted and I could see the reflection of the angel in his widened pupils, a flickering candle flame in the depths of his soul. He stopped shaking.

"*Afipneezo*," the creature said, voice reverberating around us. What did that mean? The light leaned forward and placed a chaste kiss on Rick's lips.

Rick sat up, reaching for the light, but the angel backed away. He leaped to his feet to follow. The angel shook its head. "I will," he promised, although I hadn't heard the angel ask him to do anything.

"What is that thing, Polina?" I whispered.

"I don't know," she said, voice cracking through her tears. "I've never seen anything like that. I've never felt anything like it."

"It's pure light."

"It's pure love."

"An angel."

"Looks like one, but I've never heard of them interfering in Hecate's affairs."

As quickly as it had come, the angel retreated, pausing only to bow to Isabella's remains. The light funneled back into the heavens, returning from whence it came. In its absence, Monk's Hill seemed cold and dreary, like all of the love had been drained from the landscape.

Rick stared into the sky for a moment, his loss evident on his fallen expression. All at once, he formed a fist and punched it into the earth. The ground quaked again, and iron spindles shot up around the border of the cemetery. They stabbed out of the dirt, one after another, surrounding Monk's Hill. Once in place, their tops knit into a fence, the fence I recognized as the border of my hellmouth. The border of Monk's Hill Cemetery glowed red and then faded.

"He's using magic," I said. "The angel gave him the element."

When the fence was in place, Rick climbed the hill to Isabella's remains. The fire under her had been extinguished, although I wasn't sure when this had happened, whether it was the earthquake or the appearance of the angel that put out the flames. Regardless, nothing was left of Isabella but black ash, a grainy dark sculpture where the woman once was. Rick reached out to touch her face, fingers trembling and jaw

tight with fought back tears. On contact, she came apart.
A chunk of her cheek broke off and tumbled down his
fingertips, setting off a chain reaction. Her ear dissolved,
blowing away on the wind. He sandwiched her head
between his open palms, trying to hold her together, but
his efforts backfired. The remains of her face sifted
through his fingers. There were no bones, no skull. The
fires of hell had reduced everything that was Isabella to
black flakes that took to the wind. From the top down, she
blew apart, black pieces twisting around Rick's body, until
there was nothing left between his hands but the stake.

The howl of pain Rick released broke my heart. It
started as a human sob but quickly changed into a
preternatural cry, the beastly moan of an injured animal.
He shifted as easily as I'd ever seen him, and when he was
done, his beast spread its wings and took to the sky.

I wept, Polina squeezing my hand in support.

"We have to go," she said.

I moaned as a strong case of vertigo had me grabbing
my head. I had a brief sense of drowning, a moment of
blackness, and then I was back in the room across from
Polina. The silver liquid between us sank and re-formed
into the tray. As it did, it exposed my ring, which spun
like a top at the center of the hardening metal. It slowed
and fell, spiraling to a stop.

"Heaven and earth, what did we just witness?" Polina
asked me.

"I don't know." I reached for the ring but snatched my hand back when it burned my fingers. "It had to have been an angel."

"I hope not."

"Why?"

"Because if an angel's touch is what Rick is missing, I have no idea how to make that happen again for him."

CHAPTER 16
Things That Make You Go EEK!

I was still trying to make sense of what we'd seen in the platter when screams rang out from the bar. Polina rose from her place on the floor and rushed to the door, throwing it open in time for Poe and Hildegard to barrel into the small room.

"What's going on?" I asked.

"Goblins. They're here," Poe said.

We rushed into the hall to find Julius speeding toward us. "We've got to get you out of here. Now!"

"Wait. Rick! He's in the bedroom."

Julius waved at Poe. "You, go get the caretaker."

For once, Poe didn't argue.

"You two. Come with me. My vampires can hold them back, but not for long." Julius gripped my upper arm and dragged me toward the end of the hall, Polina and Hildegard close behind. The vampire led me inside a room I presumed was once servants' quarters in the old building. There was a dumbwaiter in the wall. He slid the door open. "Get in."

"Are you kidding me? This thing must be a hundred years old!"

"This lowers into the kitchen. The kitchen has a freezer. At the back of the freezer is a trap door to a secret passageway out of the building," he said. "You must go alone if you wish for me to show your caretaker and familiar the way out."

"Will we even fit?" Polina asked.

Julius snorted. "You'll fit. In fact, two women can fit quite adequately."

"How can you know that?" I asked. "Never mind. I don't want to know."

The thought of climbing into the small space made me shiver. Julius was right. There was plenty of room. Though once inside, I couldn't stand or sit comfortably. I hunched, squatting over my tiptoes. Polina slid in on her knees beside me. She fit, but there wasn't enough room for her to turn around. Her owl wedged its body between us before Julius closed the door, and we began to descend.

A few seconds later, the lift stopped. Polina nudged my hand and brought a finger to her lips. I quieted my breath and listened. Nothing. Slowly, silently, I lifted the door. We were in the back of an industrial-style kitchen.

I contorted my body to stick one leg out, cringing as my shifting weight made the slightest sound of bending metal. Feeling for the floor, I stretched until my toes met linoleum, then squeezed the rest of me out. I helped

Polina and her owl do the same, before closing the door and sending the lift back up, in case Julius needed it for Rick and Poe.

Looking left, then right, I rounded the stainless steel counter. Polina drew her wand, and I felt for Nightshade, taking comfort in the brush of my fingers against her hilt. I'd tucked Tabetha's wand inside her sheath. If we ran into trouble, I was ready.

A knocking behind us made me jump into Polina. She gave me a little shake and pointed back at the dumbwaiter. The sound was the lift coming to a stop on the second floor. I released a deep breath, until a clank from the front of the kitchen had me ducking behind the counter. From around the edge, I saw a black silhouette enter, a male goblin, bow drawn. He scanned the room, and Polina pulled my head back behind the stainless steel cupboards. Straight ahead, I could see the door to the freezer. I nudged Polina and pointed at it.

I was about to run for it when Polina pointed at the reflection in the stainless steel cabinets across from us. The goblin was drifting toward us, searching behind each counter. Two more and he'd be on top of us. We'd never make it to the freezer. Her eyes widened, and she spread her hands.

Thinking fast, I looked back in the direction we'd come. There was a pot rack near the dumbwaiter. It would have to do. I took a deep breath and blew. An unnatural wind knocked the pots and pans together on the rack.

The goblin shifted, jogging toward the noise. We didn't waste any time. Sprinting for the freezer, I opened it enough for us to slip through, a quiet process compared to the banging pans. Hildegard's eyes glowed as I closed us into the dark freezer. With no window in the door, it was the only light. Shivering in the icy darkness, I used a little power to ignite a flame in my palm. Polina's face came into view first, followed by Hildegard. I pivoted, looking for the escape hatch and had to cover my mouth to keep from screaming.

Polina didn't fare as well. At the sight of the dead man strung up by his ankles from the ceiling, she let out a yelp before realizing her mistake and biting her lip. I was sure the walls of the freezer would muffle the sound, but I was also sure goblin hearing was better than human. We were on borrowed time. I shouldered around the body and searched the back of the freezer. No door.

"Fuck. Is this even the right freezer?" I muttered under my breath. Something strange caught my eye, a crate of dill pickles stacked in the corner. "Help me," I whispered, tugging at the crate.

She grabbed the other side. "Are you sure it's back here?"

"Nobody freezes pickles."

I had to extinguish my flame temporarily in order to use both hands to pull, but working together we slid the crate back. Sure enough, there was a small door underneath. It was frozen shut.

"Fire," Polina said.

I directed the flame in my hand toward the ice while she melted the lock on the door. We barely had it open when the door to the freezer jostled. Crouched behind the pickle crate, I couldn't see if it opened. I slid into the hole, dropping to a rough-hewn floor. Polina and Hildegard followed, silently lowering the door above her head. We listened for several minutes, but if anyone had followed us into the freezer, it did not appear they'd found the trap door behind the dead body and the pickles.

"Should I solder it closed?" Polina whispered.

"No, Rick and Poe might need it to get out."

By the light of the flame in my hand, we stood shoulder to shoulder, facing a root- filled tunnel that stunk of death.

She gritted her teeth and motioned to Hildegard. The owl took off down the passageway. We waited. I glanced at the door above me, heart pounding. When Hildegard returned, Polina's face lit up. She gestured for me to follow her and took off. Over packed dirt, wood beams, and the occasional bones, we navigated the tunnel to a crude stone stairway.

"Where do you think it leads?" Polina asked.

"Only one way to find out."

We jogged to the top and Polina nudged the door open with her shoulder.

From the cold, filthy tunnel, we emerged into an office space decorated with warm wood and stained glass. Not only did I recognize the office, but I recognized the man sitting behind the desk, staring at us with a scowl.

"Logan," I whispered.

He folded his arms across his chest. "What the fuck did you two do to my wall?"

* * * * *

Once the door closed behind us, it disappeared into the wall of Logan's office. "As good as an enchantment," Polina said, feeling for the seam.

I wondered if this was how Gary had reached Logan to compel his cooperation in getting my things. I decided not to bring up the topic. Some things are better left unsaid.

A brief explanation later, we climbed into a booth at the back of Valentine's. It was past closing time, and the restaurant was empty.

"So Rick and Julius are still over there?" Logan asked.

"I think so. We were separated. Poe is with them too. Maybe we should circle back." I wrung my hands.

"Give them a few minutes," Polina said. "Nobody knows that place better than Julius. They'll make it out."

Logan scratched his temple. "I'd heard about the tunnels, but I never realized they were still functional."

"Julius made it sound like the vampires regularly use them to move around during the day," I said. "I didn't know either."

"A huge network of bloodsuckers thriving under the city." Polina stuck out her tongue in a yuck face at Logan.

"Thanks for the image, Polina," Logan said. "At least now I know how Julius kidnapped me when he rescued me from Tabetha." Julius had kept Logan in his safe house for a time when Tabetha had threatened to kill him. Of course, what she really wanted was to kill me. Still, I appreciated Julius keeping Logan safe. The thought made me anxious to learn the fate of the vampire, my caretaker, and my familiar.

I didn't have to worry long. There was a knock on the locked front door. Logan motioned for us to wait while he peeked behind the window shades. A moment later he unlocked the door and Poe, Rick, and Julius hurried inside.

A sigh of relief broke my lips. I couldn't help myself. I bound out of my seat and threw my arms around Rick's neck, kissing him on the cheek. "I'm so glad you're safe."

He hugged me back and stroked my hair. "I am safe, but I fear you are not."

I backed away. "What do you mean?"

Julius answered for him. "Lives were lost today, Grateful. The goblins want you dead, and they are willing to do anything and kill anyone to get to you. I've never seen anything like it. We barely made it out alive."

Rick nodded. "If it weren't for Julius convincing me to follow him through a tunnel barely large enough for a dog, we'd be dead."

"I encouraged him to mist, but he could only manage a partial transformation," Julius said. "It was enough."

"You misted?" I asked.

"Not exactly," he said.

"He softened around the edges," Julius explained.

"Well, that's something," I said encouragingly.

Rick glanced away from me. Through our connection, I could sense the process had been painful. "It's okay, Rick. It's not your fault. Polina and I think that Tabetha's persigranate poisoning did more than make you forget me; it undid part of the magic that happened after I died. The caretaker spell was never completed."

Every face turned toward me. "Polina and I went back in time. We saw the whole thing. After I died, an angel came down from heaven and completed the spell. That's the part Rick lost. Whatever the angel did is gone."

Poe, who was looking rather cozy huddled on the coatrack next to Hildegard, perked to attention. "Angels do not interfere in the realm of Hecate."

"The bird is correct," Julius said. "Angels keep to the human realm. No witch includes angels in her spells."

"I know what I saw."

Polina shook her head. "I was skeptical too, but it sure as hell looked like an angel to me. The thing was made of pure light."

"How do we find out? Is there some spell we can do to conjure angels and ask if any of their kind helped Rick in the past?"

With a scoff, Julius slid in next to Polina. "Never. No supernatural being has access to angels."

"I do," Logan said. Everyone turned to stare in awe at the only human in the group. "Not directly, of course. My mom's in heaven, and she sometimes speaks with me. I could ask her about the angel next time she visits."

Polina's eyes widened, and she grabbed Logan's hand. "Can you speak with her anytime you want? Is she here now?" The redhead's eyes darted around the room.

"Eh, no," Logan said, blushing slightly. "It's sort of a one-way call with her. She comes to me and tells me things, but I can't, um, go to her."

My shoulders sagged. "So what do we do while we're waiting for Mrs. Valentine to make an appearance?" I asked.

Silence.

Julius finally spoke up. "We seek the allegiance of a water witch, as planned. If Logan is able to use his abilities as a medium to help you restore Rick, then you can use him in the spell as the earth element. Meanwhile, we obtain the allegiance of the water element."

"Whoa," Logan said. "So you're going to do this? Try to unite the elements?"

"There's no other way out. Hecate or her goblins will eventually find and kill me if I don't." My brow furrowed and I turned to Julius. "How did the goblins find your safe house anyway?"

He rubbed the smooth skin of his jaw. "Judging by the sequence of events, I believe the maid saw the mark on your chest and took it upon herself to tell her husband, who tried to profit at our expense. They are both dead. I found them shot by goblin arrows at the entrance to the speakeasy, presumably after leading them there."

"What's on your chest?" Logan asked.

Tugging the neck of my shirt aside, I showed Logan the still-healing wound. He scowled and shook his head. I allowed the material to snap back into place.

"So… where do we find a water witch?" I asked in the awkward silence that followed.

Polina shrugged. "Anywhere there's a ton of water."

I retrieved my phone from my back pocket and did a quick search for the wettest places in the US. "Hilo, Hawaii; Annette Island, Alaska; Quillayute, Washington…"

Julius wrinkled his nose. "Avoid Quillayute. There's a family of vampires there who don't appreciate my company."

"I can't imagine why," Poe said.

Everyone laughed but Julius. I moved to the next place on the list. "Astoria, Oregon."

Polina straightened. "I know her! I know the Astoria witch. Her name is… Kendall—no, that's not right— Kendra. Yes, it's Kendra. I haven't seen her in decades."

"But you know her."

"We met during the Gold Rush. We were both vacationing there in 1849. I was there for the gold, you know, metal witch. She must have been there because of the water. They panned the gold on the riverbeds. Anyway, we tormented a few cowboys together for entertainment. I can't promise she'll remember me, but I can say she seemed like a reasonable witch."

"Astoria it is," I said. "There's only one problem. All of my credit cards and identification are in the bag I left at the safe house. I don't suppose you guys brought it with you."

"We barely escaped with our skin," Rick said.

"I can't buy a plane ticket without it," I said. "How will we get to Astoria? Walk?"

"I can lend you money for the ticket," Logan said. "But they'll never let you use it without identification, and I'm guessing Rick doesn't have any either."

"Make that three of us," Polina said. "We have the clothes on our backs. I could take us through the pipes—"

"No!" Julius and I said together. Julius grunted. "Simple. I'll compel our way onto the plane. Logan will buy our tickets."

"They scan your license," I said. "Compulsion will only get you so far."

"Leave it to me," Julius said. "We best get to the airport. I'll be useless by morning. Which brings to mind an awkward practicality, I must ask that one of you be willing to care for me in my diurnal state."

"Done," I said.

Logan stood. "Give me a minute. I have a change of clothes in the office, and I need to grab my wallet."

I shook my head. "You're not coming with us! It's too dangerous. Just lend me cash for the tickets."

He laughed. "Grateful, unless you have a charger in your bra, your phone is going to be dead in a few hours. You need me with you in case my mom comes a calling.

Besides, I already made the deposit for the night. I don't have that kind of cash here."

Rick hung his head. "I may not be of use without his help with the angel."

Julius nodded his agreement.

I didn't like including Logan. It went against everything I'd promised myself about keeping him away from danger. But I had no choice.

"You must be joking!" Polina motioned to Hildegard, and the snowy owl landed on her shoulder. "He's human. If he goes, it'll be suicide." She squinted at Logan, scanning him from head to toe. "You know you're going to die, right?"

Logan lifted the corner of his lip. "I can take care of myself, lady. And I can make my own decisions. I'm going." He stormed toward his office.

Polina turned to me. "You're not going to let him go, are you?"

"If I had any hope of changing his mind, you just obliterated that idea," I said pointedly toward Polina. "The surest way to make Logan do something is to tell him he can't. There won't be a chance in hell of talking him out of it now."

CHAPTER 17
Baggage Claim

A few hours and several tense moments with security later, I found myself nestled next to Rick on a flight from Manchester to Portland. Julius had arranged for special airport services in the form of an ogre for hire. He conveniently left Julius's coffin on the tarmac long enough for him to mist into it after he compelled our way through security. The sun rose as we took off. We'd land in the afternoon and have to take care of the vampire's body until sundown.

"Have I flown in an airplane before?" Rick stared out the window at the lightening sky.

"I don't know. You're several hundred years old, so I'd be surprised if you hadn't."

"Seems unnatural."

The plane jostled and Rick gripped the armrest until I feared he'd rip it off. "It's just turbulence," I said, placing my hand over his. "Besides, you do know you can fly, right?"

"So you tell me."

"You shifted the other night. It was painful and slow, but you did it with my help. Believe me, if this plane was going down I'd help you. We'd figure it out."

"You have greater confidence in me than I have in myself."

His frown reflected in the small round window. "Shifting wasn't what you expected."

"It was painful. Excruciating. But what made it worse was before. I wanted to be with you. My body was alive for you and then"—he shook his head—"The beast took control. I tried to stop it and it happened anyway. What if—"

"What if we can't be together without you shifting?"

He nodded.

"We always could before, Rick. I'm figuring out how to make this easier for you, for us. Polina and Logan are helping us. Trust in that. We'll figure out how to make you whole again."

He nodded but didn't meet my eyes. I stared out the window over his shoulder in silence.

"I'd do it for you," he murmured.

"Do what?"

"If this plane went down, I'd shift again and learn to fly, if it meant saving you." He glanced back at me, a ghost of a smile turning the corners of his lips.

I leaned my head on his shoulder. "I know you would."

* * * * *

When we arrived in Portland, I exited the flight hand in hand with Rick, Logan and Polina behind us. I was surprised to find a pale slip of a woman with a black bob waiting for us at the end of the jetway. She wore an airport uniform and the sign in her hands read *Grateful Knight.*

No one was supposed to know I was in Oregon. Even my ticket was purchased using a different name. I slowed my steps, allowing the crowd to drift around me.

"Who is she?" Polina asked.

"I have no idea."

"She's not goblin. I don't even think she's supernatural. Those dark circles under her eyes can only be human," Polina said.

Logan snorted. "Can we stop with the human bashing?"

Polina turned her nose up and ignored him. "What's that on her neck?"

I squinted, trying to see what Polina saw, but my eyes couldn't make it out. Luckily, Rick's vision was better than mine.

"Vampire bite," he answered. "She appears to have made an attempt to conceal it."

I sighed. "She's probably working for Julius. We have to get his body."

Bolstered by murmurs of agreement from the group, I approached the girl, noticing her listless composure and almost translucent skin. She was a vamp feedbag all right. "I'm Grateful Knight."

"Oh, good." She lowered the sign. One finger shot up to sweep a dark lock off her forehead. "You can pick up your next of kin outside of baggage. They're loading him into the car for you. A man will meet you with the keys."

"Next of kin? You mean Julius," I whispered.

Her eyes shifted nervously from side to side. "Uh, I know it's hard to say goodbye." She scratched the side of her neck. "Baggage claim." Without another word, she was gone.

* * * * *

As it turned out, a car was waiting for us outside the baggage claim area. Once we'd picked up our luggage, including two rather pissed-off familiars, an ogre handed me the keys to a lovely black hearse parked in the no parking zone.

An elderly woman exiting the building beside me hesitated at the sight of the hearse. "I am sorry for your loss, dearie," she said before climbing into a waiting cab.

I slid behind the wheel, Polina climbing into the passenger's seat beside me. Rick and Logan sat behind us, freeing Poe and Hildegard from their travel cages.

"Have you any idea how humiliating that was?" Poe said. Hildegard squawked her support at his side.

"I know, Hildie, but it was the only way. It would take you two days to fly here on your own." Polina pouted and scratched Hildegard behind her fluffy white head.

I watched the show of affection as witch and familiar reunited and glanced at Poe. He met my eyes and pooped on the backseat.

"Ew." Logan scooted toward his door. "Grateful?"

"Poe! What the hell?" I said.

"It was a long flight," he protested. "Frankly, I have no idea how Hildie is containing herself."

Polina rolled down her window and whispered to the owl, who promptly exited the vehicle. "Well, go ahead," she said to Poe. "Meet us at the hotel."

To his credit, the raven checked for my approval before following out the window.

"Where to now?" I asked, handing Rick a cocktail napkin I'd tucked in my pocket to clean up after Poe.

"Motel Astoria. It's about a two-hour drive. Take your time. We won't want to visit our sister until our muscle wakes up." She nodded toward the coffin in the back.

I turned the key and carefully pulled into traffic. "Should one of us check that he's in there? We wouldn't want to be driving off with someone's misplaced dead uncle." I giggled.

The sound of the lid lifting had me glancing over my shoulder. Rick peeked inside the coffin. There was a sizzle, some smoke, and then the lid dropped abruptly.

"It is him," Rick said sheepishly.

Logan's smirk filled my rearview mirror. "It's probably a good idea that none of us mention how he got the burn on the back of his hand, for Rick's sake."

I took the scenic route to the coast, stopping only to buy a change of clothes and some sundries outside the city. The hearse was anything but discreet. It was like driving a flashing billboard alerting others to our suspicious circumstances. Everyone stared. A few people offered their condolences. One asked quite accusingly why we'd stopped to shop with a coffin in the back. I was relieved when we were back on the road.

Twenty minutes from Astoria, it started to rain. "Uh-oh," Polina said.

"What? The rain? This is one of the wettest places in the continental US. From what I read, it rains more than it doesn't."

"We're in water witch territory," Polina said. "It could just be rain. Or it could mean Kendra knows we're here."

The rain fell harder on the top of the hearse. To me, the rhythm resembled drumming fingers. I raised an eyebrow at Polina, and she turned her face toward the roof.

"Yeah. I'm thinking she knows we're here."

CHAPTER 18
The Axe

The Motel Astoria seemed like the type of place that rented rooms by the hour, and an hour in one of their rooms was sixty minutes too long. By the time we parked under the cracked robin's egg blue sign, it was raining so hard the wipers couldn't keep up.

My phone rang, and I retrieved it from my back pocket. Logan tapped me on the shoulder before I answered.

"I'll go," he said, pointing at the motel door marked *office*. He dashed out the door.

"I'll help. I need to stretch my legs," Polina added.

I nodded as I placed the phone to my ear.

"Grateful, where the fuck are you?" my best friend, Michelle, yelled.

"Running for my life. Witchy business," I said solemnly.

"What? Are you joking?"

"Unfortunately, no. And my phone is almost out of juice, so don't be offended if it cuts off."

"Where are you? Do you need my help?"

"It's better if you don't know, Michelle. This is serious. If anyone tries to talk to you about me, try to change the subject."

"That's going to be difficult, considering."

"Considering what?"

"You had a shift yesterday at the hospital."

"Fuck!" I'd totally forgotten. Understandable given the circumstances, but since I'd already been written up for being late multiple times, a definite career no-no.

"Yeah, well, you didn't call in, and they were short-staffed. They've been trying to reach you."

"I had my phone turned off on the plane."

"You had to take a plane?"

"Just don't ask, okay? I can't say anything more. I don't want them coming after you to get to me."

"Who? What? Does Logan know?" I watched Logan through the window of the office, paying for our room. Rick frowned beside me, no doubt picking up on my general mood.

"Tell my father that I love him."

"Fuck that, Grateful. You get your shit together. This is not going to be the last time we talk, got it?" I could hear her voice crack over the line. She was crying. "I don't know what's going on, but I'm not telling your dad goodbye. There's no reason to. You are going to straighten this shit out and get home. Then I'll help you find another job."

I took a deep breath. "Another job. They're firing me. You called to tell me I'm fired."

"Well, Kathleen mentioned it to me in the context of me taking your shifts. I'm sorry, Grateful. Maybe it's for the best. The witchy stuff has been more than a full-time job lately. I'm sure Rick can help you stay afloat until you find something else. I just thought it would be easier coming from me."

"It is." Wet trails coursed down my cheeks, but I hid it from my voice. "My phone's going to die. I love you, Michelle."

"I love you too, Grateful. Fix whatever it is and come home. There are plenty of jobs out there, but not plenty of friendships like ours. Try not to worry about anything. Just fix it."

"I will." We ended our call, and I had enough time to check that I indeed had four missed voicemails from Kathleen. My phone went dead before I could listen to any of them. Just as well.

"Who was that?" Rick asked from beside me.

"My best friend," I sobbed in earnest. "I was fired from my job." I desperately needed a Kleenex, but I'd sacrificed my last paper product to clean up after Poe.

Rick wiped the back of his knuckle gently under one eye and then the other, before pulling me to his chest. "Afloat means to pay your bills, correct?"

"Correct," I murmured, not surprised his super-hearing picked up Michelle's side of the conversation.

"Don't worry. I will keep you *afloat,* as your friend calls it, until you find another job."

"You would do that for me?" I tilted my head back to look at him, still tucked into his chest.

He stroked my hair back from my face and wiped my tears away with his thumb. "I find I would do many things for you. I take care of you, yes?"

"Yes."

His eyes locked onto mine, and the intimacy was immediate. Our connection was no longer a filmy spiderweb but a braided rope. I held perfectly still, afraid if I moved I'd ruin the moment. Deliberately, he used his arm to curl me closer and lowered his mouth to mine. The kiss was soft, languid. More than sexual, way beyond a touching of lips, this kiss tasted of promise and commitment. In that moment, I was utterly held, cradled in space and time.

Bang, bang, bang. Logan's knock on the rain-drenched window interrupted the moment. He dangled a key from his fingers and pointed at room number four before jogging back under the cover of the second-floor walkway. Reluctantly, I gestured to Rick, and we followed. Logan murmured something to me as I filtered out of the rain and into the space between the bed and the dresser.

"What did you say?" I asked. "The rain was too loud."

"Julius," he said, pointing his thumb through the open door. "Do you think he's okay out there by himself?"

Polina smirked, smoothing back her wet hair. "What are the options? Do you think the local humans will be comfortable with a group of us carrying a casket into a place like this in broad daylight?"

"Listen, I don't need the attitude, lady. I was just asking the question," Logan said, dripping on the carpet.

"What's your problem?" Polina shot back.

"I'm just getting a little sick of you criticizing everything I do." Logan opened his mouth to say more, but I cut him off by clearing my throat and placing myself between them.

"Julius will be fine. I locked the doors to the hearse. Why don't you come inside?" I asked. Logan was still leaning his shoulder into the open door.

"I like to watch the rain."

Logan shot Polina one last sharp look then turned to stare at the rain sheeting over the parking lot beyond the overhang of the second-floor walkway. I didn't think it was about the rain. It was about air and space. The more the better between him and Polina.

Rick toed a stain on the carpet that looked suspiciously like blood, his nostrils flaring. "How long must we stay here?"

"Until sunset," I said. "Once Julius wakes up, we'll approach Kendra."

A crack of thunder shook the room, and Polina used the back of her hand to spread the orangey-brown curtains to see outside while avoiding Logan and the door. "If she doesn't approach us first," she said.

"Where does she live, exactly?" I asked Polina.

"I don't know for sure. I've never been to her place. But judging by the signs, she lives inside the wildlife refuge at the mouth of the Columbia River."

"What signs?" Rick asked.

"Witches always live in rural and forested areas. They don't do well in big cities, not even metal witches. The wildlife refuge is surrounded by water and out of reach of humans. It's the most likely place. Of course, there will have to be a cemetery nearby."

"If it's out of reach of humans, how do we get there?" Logan asked.

Polina shook her head and snorted. "You won't be coming. Grateful and I will have to use magic to get there, and even then it's dangerous. We're on a water witch's home turf. Kendra could crush us under a tidal wave in a heartbeat."

Lightning cracked, the light and thunder cutting off Logan's heated response. I had a feeling Kendra was listening. Could she hear us through the rain? Were we welcome here?

"I smell…" Rick poked the stain on the floor again with his toe, his nostrils flaring.

"What?" I threaded my fingers into his. "What do you smell?"

"It is like… fish. Fresh fish."

Polina's eyes widened. In a flash, she crossed the room, hooked an arm around Logan's chest, and hurled him behind her to the back of the room. I didn't have to ask why. Two scaly beasts appeared in the open doorway. Frogmen—that's what came to mind—although their scaly skin was flesh-colored, and they could pass for human from a distance. Close up, they had wide mouths and gills under each ear, but the harpoon guns in their hands seemed to be their primary mode of communication. They poked the business end at Polina and made an awful, grating croak, motioning toward the parking lot with their heads.

My redheaded sister flashed me a look of genuine fear. "Kendra invites us to her home and insists our male guests join us."

Frowning, I glanced from Rick to Logan, then at the sharp harpoons pointed at our throats.

Logan put his hands on his hips. "How can we refuse?"

CHAPTER 19
Kendra

The two frogmen ushered us out into the rain, where I had to cup my hands over my eyes just to see. A third frog joined the group with a bag of scuba-style masks, small containers attached to the front. Oxygen? I wasn't sure.

The frogman handed one to me and grunted, poking the barb of his harpoon into my chin. "Oww," I said, stepping back into Rick. "Hold your horses. I'll put it on."

"Grateful," Rick said. He turned to me and glanced down at his arm. His skin bubbled menacingly.

"Not now," I said under my breath.

He shrugged as if to suggest he had no control over it. A scaly hand with webbed fingers shook my shoulder, leaving behind a slick of oil on my shirt—quite the accomplishment in the pouring rain. I placed the mask on my head as the frogman showed us, and watched as Logan,

Rick, and Polina did the same. I could breathe easily with it on, although the respirator made it difficult to hear anything else.

With a grunt, the frogman motioned for us to slide the masks up to our foreheads. "Was that some kind of a test?" I asked. He didn't answer me.

I looked around for a transportation device. Would they take us to Kendra in a seashell? A magical surfboard? The frogmen led us to a military-style Jeep. I forced myself not to look in the direction of the hearse or to search the sky for Poe and Hildegard. If they could avoid detection, they might be our only hope if things went sour.

Rick squeezed my hand as we smashed into the backseat, four across. I could feel the energy coming off him. His beast was close to the surface, his protective instincts impossible to deny, but now was not the time for heroics. I needed to meet Kendra and enlist her alliance, not start a witchy war. I stroked his arm, trying my best to calm him. Could he even shift completely without me pulling the strings? Probably not, and maybe that was a good thing.

"Don't worry. I'll take care of you," I heard Polina say.

I turned around to tell her I could take care of myself but found she was talking to Logan, who was doing his best not to panic as the Jeep lurched into motion. A bumpy twenty-minute journey later, we reached the coast. The frogs drove us to an abandoned marina and down a boat ramp.

"What are they doing?"

"Oh shit," Logan said.

We all pulled the masks into position as the Jeep plunged into the ocean. The vehicle filled with saltwater and soon the only thing keeping me from floating to the ceiling was my seat belt. Rick squeezed my hand. Seaweed masked the windows and the occasional fish wriggled in the mass. As I watched the bubbles rise between us, and saw the small container of oxygen connected to the mouthpiece, I wondered how much air we had. I didn't doubt it was enough to take us to Kendra. I questioned whether there was enough to get us out again.

I turned at Logan's muffled scream. The skull of a skeleton poked out from the hull of a sunken ship beside us. I could feel the dead here. Lots of them, and they weren't mine. This was Kendra's graveyard.

Slowly, we ascended, breaking from the seafloor and driving toward a bright light. The Jeep broke the surface and the water drained away from the interior. I tried to draw a breath through the respirator and got nothing. Breathless, I pulled it off my head. I was right. This was a one-way ticket. My canister was empty. Beside me, the others removed their masks, one by one.

We arrived inside a brightly lit cavern with iridescent walls covered in crustaceans and anemone. Rudely, the frogmen pulled us from the vehicle and prodded us forward with their harpoons. We followed obediently through winding passages of stone until modern conveniences increasingly replaced natural wonders. A carpet, a light, a chest of drawers. The frogmen stopped us in a quaint sitting room decorated in beach décor, complete with a shell lamp.

"Do we wait here?" I asked. No waiting was required.

"I'm sorry I can't offer you refreshments. You caught me off guard when you came into my ward without permission." Kendra, the witch of Astoria, walked into the room with the straight back and squared shoulders of a ballerina. Lanky in stature, she sported a short pixie cut of black hair and eyes as blue as the waters we'd traversed to get to her. Her sophisticated sheath dress was the color of a sand dollar. She circled Logan, her gaze lingering on his lower body in a way that made me uncomfortable.

"Hi. I'm Logan." He thrust one hand toward her. She didn't shake it.

"Is the human a gift or some kind of a pet?"

"He's with us," I said. "Not a gift."

She turned her attention on Rick. "And this one?"

"Not a gift either," Rick answered for himself, stepping closer to me.

"My caretaker," I explained.

Her eyebrows rose. "Caretaker. I haven't seen a witch with a caretaker in a century."

"Now you have."

She inspected the two of us with her icy blue gaze. "What brings you to my ward?"

Polina removed the mask from her forehead and shook out her long red hair, still wet from our journey. "Do you remember me, Kendra? I'm Polina, the

Smuggler's Notch witch. We met vacationing during the Gold Rush."

With a slight narrowing of her eyes, Kendra gave her head a little shake. "Sorry. The 1840s are nothing but a blur. I was into some rough magic back then. Anyway, this doesn't look like a social visit."

"Uh, no."

"I'm sorry to surprise you like this," I said. "My name is Grateful Knight, and I came because I need your help."

Kendra sank into a cushioned rattan armchair in the corner. "My help? Why on earth would you need my help?"

"It's a long story." I bent my knees to sit on the sofa beside her but she objected.

"I didn't invite you to sit."

I straightened my knees. Her expression wasn't angry exactly, but terse. She occupied the beachy rattan like a queen on her throne, and perhaps she was. This was her territory. We were at her mercy.

"What are you?" she asked. "My senses are twitching. You are a witch for sure, but there is something more to you, yes?"

I started talking. I told her about Tabetha, the goblins, and even Hecate, although I twisted the story a bit to imply that the goddess wanted me to unite the elements in order to set things right. During my story, my hand had risen to cover the mark on my chest. I hoped it looked like a natural movement, hand over heart, a vow of honesty.

She took it all in without saying a word.

"I'm here because we need your help to unite the elements, so I can cast off Tabetha's power. I don't want it. I don't need it. I want to make things right again," I concluded.

Kendra leaned back in her chair, eyes darting to Polina. "And you have agreed to help her?"

Polina nodded. "She's a good witch, Kendra. She only killed Tabetha to protect herself. She never meant to break the natural law."

"Yes, well, despite what you've said, I highly doubt the goddess gave you permission to unite the elements. While I believe you when you say that someone wants you dead, I do not believe that someone is the goblins. Goblins are mercenaries. You've admitted to me that you've broken the natural law and have power over two elements." Kendra's fingers stroked a large conch shell on the side table next to her. I wasn't sure if water witches used wands, but I was relatively sure the conch was a magical object of some kind. One I didn't want to tangle with. "Why should I believe that you two aren't colluding to kill me to get what you want?"

"We came here to solicit your help. If the answer is no, that's fine. We'll find someone else," I said.

"Are you denying that you deceived me about having Mother's permission to unite the elements? If you lied about that, how can I trust anything you say?" Kendra squeezed the conch and the sound of the ocean powered through the room.

I wasn't the only one who noticed the conch. Polina placed her hands on her hips and shrugged her shoulders with a huff. "Mother was the one who gave Grateful permission to kill Tabetha. She opened her up to this and now doesn't want to live with the consequences."

"You might think you'll be on her good side if you kill me," I said. "But don't be fooled. You'll be the next on her hit list."

Kendra removed her hand from the conch. "I'm not going to kill you."

A collective sigh of relief came from the four of us.

"But I'm not going to help you. Whether or not your intentions are pure, no witch in her right mind would help you." She stood and smoothed her dress. "It's too risky."

I frowned but nodded. "I appreciate your honesty. If you could give us a ride back to our motel, we'll be on our way."

"Of course. Simply leave the human as a gift to me, and I'll have my frogs return you to your room."

Logan, who'd been passively listening to this point, perked up. "Excuse me? The human is not theirs to give."

I opened my mouth to protest, but Polina beat me to it. "He's with us," she said.

Kendra shook her head and pointed at her chest. "I should be compensated for my time. You came into *my* ward. I had to bring you here. The least you can do is leave the human."

"Does anyone care what the human thinks of this plan?" Logan yelled.

"No!" Polina and Kendra said together.

Logan's mouth dropped open, positively stunned.

Kendra hooked her arm under his. "Come, my pet. You're mine now."

"I said no!" Polina yelled, and the walls shook and cracked with her anger. A trickle of water ran down the interior.

"What are you doing?" Kendra snapped.

"High mercury content in the water," Polina said through her teeth. "Return the human."

"I don't think so. I think I'll keep him." Kendra pulled Logan toward her.

"He's ours." Polina pulled him back.

"You know, I do remember you, Polina. You pulled this same shit with that boy by the river in 1849."

"That boy wasn't interested in you, Kendra. Not to mention he was useless with gold fever. Believe me, he wasn't a catch. He made a choice and I just followed through. You were better off—"

"Spare me. You knew exactly what you were doing. You cast a love spell on that human boy. He didn't stand a chance."

Logan glanced between the two witches. "No need to fight over me. The human can make up his own mind." He jerked his arm away from Kendra and stepped to Rick's side, as if to gain masculine solidarity.

Rick cleared his throat and said, "The human has made his choice. We thank you for your time."

I flashed a smile at my caretaker and followed his lead. We had definitely overstayed our welcome. "Goodbye, Kendra." I turned to leave the way we came, one eye on Kendra.

"How do you plan to get out without my help?" she said evenly.

"We'll figure it out."

Polina walked faster toward the corridor, urging us forward.

Kendra shook her head and reached for the conch. "Oh, I couldn't be so rude. Let me show you out."

My eyes widened as she lowered her fingers to the shell.

"Run!" Polina said. Rick grabbed my arm and pulled me forward, pushing Logan and Polina ahead of us into the hallway. We weren't fast enough. A tsunami roared down the cavern behind Kendra, a mighty rush of water that moved around her as if she were protected inside a bubble of magic, and powered into us. I had just enough time to take a breath of air before ten thousand gallons of ocean sent me shooting through the corridor.

My head slammed against the barnacle-encrusted wall, and I was washed away into total blackness.

CHAPTER 20
New Growth

Strong arms lifted me from the blackness, out of the cold, wet, deep, and dark. I sputtered and coughed, as my savior laid me out near the waters edge, tipped me on my side, and patted between my shoulder blades as I cleared my lungs of water. My eyes fluttered open. Still in a fit of coughing, I rolled flat again, sharp stones poking into my back and head.

Rick's face hovered above me. "Thank the goddess."

I raised eyebrows. "Believe me, if it were up to the goddess, I'd be dead. Thank you. *You* saved me."

He pulled me into his lap as if I weighed nothing and cradled me in his arms, stroking my hair and pressing his lips to my cheek. I shivered, my teeth clanking together noisily. "You need my blood." He raised his wrist to my mouth.

I kissed it gently. "No… no, I'll be okay. Just give me a minute." I didn't want to waste his strength, especially if

175

he needed to shift to protect us. I sat up in his lap and looked around. We were alone on the Oregon beach at night. I was frigid, and the full moon gave off just enough light to see his outline in the dark and fog. "Where are the others?"

"I could only hold you," Rick said sadly. "It was all I could do."

I placed a hand on his cheek and pecked him on the lips. "It's not your fault. Polina can take care of herself." Privately, I hoped Polina had taken care of Logan as well. I braced myself on Rick's knee and shoulder and allowed him to help me to my feet "Polina! Logan!" I stage-whispered toward the foggy water.

"Relax, Grateful," Julius's voice came from a distance, somewhere within the fog. "I have them both."

"Where are you?"

"Down the beach. To your left."

Rick sidled up to me and took my hand. "I see them. Come."

A few hundred feet down the beach, I kneeled by Logan's body and assessed his vitals. He was alive and breathing but had a nasty bump on the head. Polina had it worse. Her outer arms and back were shredded.

"Fortunately, vampires don't need to breathe." Julius brushed a wet lock of hair back from his pale forehead, his blue eyes giving off their own light. "It took me some time to track you here. I couldn't have done it without our bond, but when I woke I heard your blood call out to me.

And then, when it was clear you were unharmed, I decided you'd be displeased if I didn't rescue these two."

"Very displeased," I said, bristling at his cold demeanor. "You did the right thing."

He flashed fang. "Good enough for a reward?" He shifted closer to me, his large nocturnal eyes raking my shivering flesh.

"What kind of reward?"

"I am hungry, Grateful."

Rick growled, a low, menacing rumble from the center of his chest.

"Sorry, Julius. No."

He hissed. "I should have let them drown." He thrashed toward Logan's throat.

I placed a hand on his chest to stop him, and he instantly calmed at my touch. He lowered his nose to my inner arm and inhaled. He was starving. His skin was chalky white, and he couldn't close his mouth completely over his extended fangs. I had to offer him something.

"I'm, uh, injured, and I need all my blood," I said. "But this is a forest preserve. Go hunt. Come back when you've drained a deer or two."

He scowled but obeyed me, racing across the beach and into the tree line.

"He's bound to you?" Rick asked.

"Unfortunately, yes."

"The same as I am bound to you?"

I met his gray eyes. "No. Nothing like that. Our connection is purposeful because we love... loved each other." I smiled weakly. "Julius was an accident. As soon as magically possible, I plan to sever the bond."

Rick gave a curt nod. I leaned toward him and kissed him gently on the mouth. A fit of coughing from Polina separated us.

"Polina, are you okay?"

She opened her green eyes and sat up abruptly, holding the bodice of her shredded top to her chest. "Logan!"

"He's right here," I said, pointing to his unconscious body beside her.

She raked her gaze over him, then patted her bodice and pockets until she found her wand tucked into the top of one boot. "Will he live?"

"I think so. Just knocked out. Pulse is strong. Respiration's normal. He might have a concussion."

"Good," she murmured. With a flick of her wrist, the decorative buttons on her corset melted and oozed to stitch up the torn cloth. In no time, her outfit was whole again, and her skin had begun to mend itself.

I sat back on my heels. "I thought you weren't concerned with the fate of a simple human."

She snorted. "I'm not, but hell if I'm going to let that bitch have him—dead or alive. Besides, we need him to channel the beyond and find the angel who helped Rick."

"Right." I had a feeling there was more to Polina's interest in Logan than thwarting another witch or helping me. She couldn't keep her eyes off him. But then, I had some experience with Logan's magnetism. Immune to it now, I had no feelings for him other than friendship, but I could not deny that there was something about him that set witchy senses aflutter. I assumed it was the supernatural recipe that gave him the power of a medium, the power to touch that area of spirituality we couldn't. Whatever it was, I was willing to bet Polina was more affected than she let on.

A groan parted Logan's lips, and he raised one hand to rub the bump on his head.

"That's it. I officially hate witches," he said as he sat up between us.

I must have made a face because he tacked on, "Except for you two, of course."

"Of course," I murmured.

Polina ignored the comment. "We should get out of here." She eyed the ocean's lapping waves. "We're too close to the water."

I nudged Rick, and he helped me get Logan to his feet. We each supported one of his arms and limped toward the forest.

"Julius," I called toward the trees. He emerged, mouth covered in blood, holding the broken body of a doe under his arm like a football.

"Ugh," Logan said with a wince. "That guy has issues."

"Where's the car?" I asked.

He pointed to the right. "About a mile west."

"Meet us when you're finished. We need to implement plan B."

Julius nodded and melded back into the shadow of the woods.

"What's plan B?" Rick asked me.

"I have no idea."

* * * * *

We didn't return to the room in Astoria. Instead, once Julius was finished, we called Poe and Hildegard to us, loaded everyone into the hearse, and drove east. Rick made himself comfortable in the passenger's seat as the miles drifted by.

"Where will we go now?" he asked, playing with the radio.

"I thought we'd head into the Rockies, maybe try for an earth witch there. I need a break from the water for a while." I smiled at him, but he didn't find anything funny about my comment.

"Why do you need an earth witch? I thought I held the earth element."

"You might... or you might not. If Tabetha's spell rolled back my caretaker spell to the point where your memory ends, then you never received the magic from the angel. We're not sure exactly how it works, but since you haven't fully accessed your power, I'm not sure you'll work in the ceremony."

He adjusted himself in the seat beside me. "I've shifted now, and been strong enough to save you twice."

"Thank you. Rick, you're amazing. Considering everything you've been through, I can't believe how gracefully you're taking all of this."

"But I don't remember caretaker magic, and you're afraid my power won't work," he said.

I sighed. "Yes."

His head rolled against the headrest to look out the window. "Our time would be better spent securing a water witch's alliance," Julius said from the backseat. "We could attempt the spell with Rick if we had to and only waste the energy on another witch if it didn't work."

Logan was asleep next to Julius, a state that concerned me given his blow to the head. Still, I couldn't bear to wake him up. He was exhausted.

Polina leaned forward until her face was next to mine. "The vampire is right. We should try Hilo or maybe one of the witches of the Great Lakes."

My eyelids drooped and a weight formed over my chest, making it hard to breathe. At once, I felt both torn in two and compressed, the problems ahead of me piling into an insurmountable mountain. With a jerk of the wheel and a pump of the brakes, I pulled over to the side of the road and parked the car.

"What are you doing?" Julius asked.

"I'm sore and tired and I need to think," I said.

"I can drive," Polina offered.

I opened the door and slammed it behind me. "Give me a minute. I need some air. I just…" I faced Rick, Polina, Julius, and Logan, all of them waiting for direction from me, waiting to risk their lives again for me, and shook my head. "I need to be alone." I turned away before the first tears fell and rushed toward the trees.

The forest off the side of the road was a refuge, a dark tangle of vegetation that seemed to hum to the wood witch in me. It was a cold night, but I took off my shoes and walked barefoot. Night air circled me, a soft breeze that warmed at my request. I'd seen Tabetha do this, call the spring with every step. It was already spring, and it didn't take much to warm the grass under my feet and bring the temperature around me to a pleasant seventy degrees.

Into the trees, I escaped. It was less of a stroll as a full-out run. I leaped into the arms of the dense patch of forest and breathed deeply of pine and spruce. I stroked my fingers over needles and bark and nestled into a womb of giant sequoias. Moss grew under my feet, and ferns brushed my calves. When my legs grew tired, I lay down on my back in a soft cradle of moss between two massive roots. The roots belonged to a type of tree I could not name in the dark. My magic had brought me here. It felt safe.

I stared up through the branches at the starry sky and let out a deep contented breath.

"How may I serve you, forest queen?" I jolted at the sound of a woman's voice and saw a dark, curly head break from the bark above me. A tree sprite, old and gnarled, glowed subtly green in the moonlight.

"Oh! I don't need anything. I'm sorry to disturb you. Just wanted a place to rest. Do you mind?"

"Of course not. The magic coming off you is fertilizer for an ancient soul like me."

A rogue worry struck me. "Am I in the territory of another wood witch? I don't mean to cause any trouble."

"Heavens no. No humans out here to protect. The closest Hecate is twenty miles east, and she's not a wood anyway."

I swallowed, afraid to ask. "What kind of witch is she?"

"The water variety, I believe. New witch. Called after the untimely destruction of the last by the hands of a demon. Barely casting her first spells, I've heard. Nothing to worry about."

I turned that news over in my head. A new witch might be easier to convince than Kendra. "What town did you say she was in?"

"She's the Mount Coffin witch, in Longview, Washington."

"Mount Coffin?"

"Skillute burial ground. Old dead there. She'll be powerful when she comes into her own."

"Thank you. Maybe I'll stop by and welcome her into the sisterhood." I linked my fingers behind my head and lay back in the soft moss.

The sprite laughed. "I'm sure she'd like that. Oh!" I startled when she shrieked and retreated into her tree.

Searching the forest, I found the source of her fear. A few yards away, Rick leaned against a tree, watching me.

"It's all right," I called to the sprite's bark. "He's my caretaker."

She didn't respond verbally, but above me, a tiny feather of light drifted down, and then another. I caught one in my palm. A seed with a dandelion-soft umbrella of fuzz that caught the slightest breeze. Another and another drifted over me in the moonlight. I smiled at Rick. "Looks like she's making it snow for us."

"I was worried about you," he said.

"About me? I can take care of myself."

He approached and lowered beside me, resting his back against the mighty tree trunk. "Why should you have to?"

I smiled at the thought that Rick felt responsible for me. We'd come a long way these past weeks. "It was rude of me to leave everyone waiting in the car, but I needed…"

"To be among your element. Fresh air, growing things." He ran his hand over the moss between us.

"Exactly."

"You were always this way. Isabella had a name for every plant in the woods and its purpose. She would just as well swim in the pond than take a proper bath, and the stars were her favorite canopy."

"I'm not Isabella, Rick," I said with an exasperated sigh. "I don't have those memories."

"And I don't have the memories you have of me. I know you are not Isabella, but it seems we remain the same people we were to each other."

I turned on my side and trailed my fingers over the back of his hand. "How do you mean?"

"You were brave and strong then, and you are brave and strong now." He wrapped his arms around his knees and stared up at the stars. "And I find myself haunted by you, the same as I was haunted by her."

"Haunted? Like a spirit that needs vanquishing?"

"No. Like being alone in a room the morning after Christmas, when you can almost hear the laughter and joy that occurred the night before. Like knowing the sun is about to rise." He licked his bottom lip. "The care of you is at the core of me. It feels like it always has been and always will be the thing that makes my heart beat and my chest rise with each breath."

With my head propped up on my elbow, I went for broke. "Do you love me, Rick?"

Somewhere a cricket started to sing and night sounds magnified in the silence. A frog croaked, an animal scurried through the brush, a breeze rustled the leaves above us.

"It seems inevitable that I will love you."

"But you don't yet."

"There hasn't been enough time to know for sure."

I lowered my head to my arm and rolled onto my back to look up at the stars. Loving me was inevitable. That was something. There was hope. If I survived all this, things might go back to normal. Presuming the Goblin Trinate didn't shoot me, and I wasn't obliterated by another witch. And assuming I could shed the extra element inside me, and the goddess Hecate didn't strike me down in some other fashion. And that I was able to stay in my home, considering I'd been fired from my job. If all that came together, and Rick learned to love me again, things might be all right.

My eyes burned with my need to cry at my pitiful existence.

"I don't love you yet, Grateful, but I hunger for you," Rick whispered, turning from the stars to look at me. "All I can think about is touching you, the taste of your blood, the feel of your hair in my fingers."

I froze, mentally squashing my pity party. Did he just say he wanted me? "Then why don't you touch me?" I whispered, afraid if I said it too loudly I'd jinx the mood.

"I'm afraid."

"Afraid you'll shift?"

"I don't want to hurt you."

I tugged at his arm gently. "I think I can help. I can teach you how to control it."

He held back. I could feel him fighting our connection, struggling against his need for me.

"You don't wish to wait?" He swallowed. "For love? For marriage?"

I shook my head. My voice was thick as pinesap and desperate. "I can't, Rick. I need you. I need you too much."

CHAPTER 21
Bom Chicka Wah Wah

If there had been any doubt or hesitancy on his part about being with me, I couldn't sense it through our connection anymore. Perhaps it shattered or maybe grew too thin and simply dissolved. Rick leaned over and kissed me, a soft, lingering kiss that made my heart dance. I wrapped both arms around his neck and rolled, scooping my knee under his hip and coaxing his body on top of me. He propped himself on his elbows, cradling my head in his hands.

His kiss grew more fervent. I dug my fingers beneath the hem of his shirt and worked my way to his chest. He groaned into my mouth and broke from the kiss just long enough for me to pull the shirt over his head. My shirt came off next and was a brutal reminder of my filthy state. The cotton was stiff with seawater. My hair was a wild, tangled nest, and I was sure I stunk like seaweed and ocean.

Rick, on the other hand, smelled as he always did—like the night. Rain, cedar, honeysuckle. He had a layered and complex scent that oozed from his skin. I couldn't get enough. I went to work on the fly of his jeans, struggling with the button until he helped me. My hands shook with need. He might as well have been made of heroin; my addiction was complete.

When I touched him, my hand worked between our pressed bodies. His kiss deepened and struck blood. His jaw had elongated, and his fangs had dropped, the beast rising to the surface. He pulled back and licked his lips.

"Shhh," I said. "It's okay. I can handle him." I ran fingers through his hair and stroked the back of his head. "Relax." Closing my eyes, I focused on our connection. Where I'd been anxious to bring about Rick's first shift, this time I pressed the beast back. Not entirely. I wanted Rick to learn to control it on his own. My interference was the equivalent of a velvet chain, a gentle reminder for the animal to remain at bay while I dealt with the man.

He sighed over me, and I opened my eyes.

"Better?" I asked.

The corner of his mouth lifted, and he answered by kissing me again. Before his memory loss, Rick would have had me naked and panting by now. I needed to remember this Rick needed time. To him, it was our first time. I rolled him onto his back and stood up to remove the rest of my clothing while he removed his. He watched me with reverence, the moonlight playing across his skin at an angle that made him half light and half dark.

Once I was naked, I stood over him, then lowered myself to my knees. I crawled up his body until I met his lips again and circled my hips over the tip of his erection. I wanted him so badly my body ached, but I wouldn't force him.

"Are you sure?" I asked as a hint of fear came through between us. "Are you having second thoughts?"

In response, he dug his fingers into my hair and raised his hips, penetrating me. Sex with Rick was never normal or even average, but the time we'd waited to connect had rendered my senses raw. For a moment, my head spun with pleasure at the feel of him. The air thickened with power, and the forest seemed to glory in it. As I started to rise and fall above him, the branches around us grew at an unusual rate. A vine sprouted near our heads and transformed into a rose bush that bloomed in the moonlight. One singing cricket turned into five hundred. Birds or bats fluttered overhead, and the leaves around us rustled with animal visitors, attracted by the power.

I barely noticed. My entire focus was on the man under me, who tensed and relaxed as his beast fought for control. *You stay where you are*, I told the beast through our connection, *and I'll give you a reason to behave.*

I increased my pace, propped myself on his chest and unhinged my hips. His hands coasted over my breasts, up my back, and down to cradle my thighs. The blissful edge came into view, and I pitched myself over without hesitation. He followed, shattering under me.

The skin of his neck shimmered with sweat in the moonlight, and I couldn't resist. I struck, biting until I drew blood. Sweet ambrosia washed over my tongue. He stiffened at the bite, then relaxed, breathing deeply as I swallowed. When I'd had my fill, I lifted my torso to see him better, still straddling him hip to hip. "Was that okay?"

He looked at me from under hooded eyes and grinned like he held a sweet, dark secret. Sitting up, he pressed his chest into mine and wrapped my hair around one of his hands. "Oh yes," he growled and struck my bared vein.

Memory or no memory, Rick was a fast learner and wickedly creative. We were together again, one body. I was confident, in time, the rest would come.

* * * * *

In the wee morning, sore and sated from unmeasured hours of lovemaking, Rick and I dressed and returned to the car. It was still dark, and I hoped to reach a motel before sunrise and find a safer place to store Julius for the day.

"It's about time," Polina said. She was leaning against the outside of the car next to Logan, looking decidedly pissed with her arms crossed and her familiar squawking angrily from her shoulder.

"Sorry, I, uh…"

Logan rolled his eyes. "Everyone knows exactly what you were, uh, doing, Grateful. Even I could feel the power coming off you two. It was like standing at the edge of a nuclear test zone out here. Julius had to take off in the opposite direction to keep from ripping someone's throat out. Poe and Hildegard caught up to us and kept going. Said it was overwhelming."

"Sorry," I said again.

"Look, I'm relieved you're all powered up," Polina said, "but we need a plan. We're not safe here. Everyone's hungry and tired. It's time to move and come up with plan B."

I stared at Logan. "Anything? Has your mother appeared to you at all?"

"No. Nothing." He rubbed his chin. "I'm trying; I really am. Connections are open. She just has nothing to say to me."

Rick placed his hands on his hips. "Perhaps the magic will return to me in time, without the angel."

"Maybe," I said. He did seem to be healing, but I couldn't separate our new relationship from the last. Our connection was stronger. He had more control. Although I had no way of testing the magic within him. I called for Julius and Poe and climbed behind the wheel. A few minutes later a reluctant vampire joined us in the hearse, as did my familiar and Hildegard.

"Feeling better, oh Mistress of the Morgue?" Poe said with a low chuckle.

"I need your help, Poe. My phone is dead, and we need to find Longview, Washington." Dead was an understatement. My phone was likely corroded with seawater beyond repair.

Poe bristled. "It's back toward the river. Out of Kendra's ward, I'm sure, but not beyond her power."

"Trust me."

Poe took to the sky. I started the car and followed.

"Are you sure you know what you're doing?" Polina asked.

Rick threaded his fingers into mine and squeezed his support.

"Of course not," I said. "But this is the best chance we've got at the moment. I'll explain on the way."

* * * * *

We arrived in Longview just before dawn and checked into the Red Mound motel on the edge of town. We managed to get Julius and his coffin tucked away without much notice, aside from a drunk who was sleeping near the pool. He raised eyebrows at the sight of us carrying the casket up the stairs, but if it worried him, he didn't say anything.

Once Julius was tucked in for the day, we left a *do not disturb* sign on the door and walked to a Trader's Waffle House down the street. Over fluffy Belgian waffles covered in chunky blueberry-peach syrup, Polina finally challenged my plan.

"The tree sprite said the witch was new, not that she was dumb. She's going to question your motives."

"Not if we're convincing. We show up at her door offering to help her train—to take her under our wing. It's better that there are two of us. We can say we are interested in a sisterhood, a support group."

Logan took a deep swig of his coffee. "If she's new, she's probably weak. You two should just take her. Throw a potato sack over her head and get the job done."

"Logan!" I said. "We can't kidnap her. Gah, you're starting to sound like Julius."

"Why can't you kidnap her? Temporarily. Not to hurt her but to force her to do the spell."

"Well, I'm sure she has to participate willingly," I said.

Polina shook her head. "Not as far as I know. I'm pretty sure if you are touching her and she's breathing, the two of us should be able to draw on her element. If she's struggling, she could make it difficult, but we could drug her."

"Oh." I paused, considering the possibilities.

Rick, who was pretending to enjoy a cup of coffee despite the fact he didn't need to ingest normal food, looked at me through the corner of his eye.

"What do you think?" I asked him.

In that quiet and dark way that I'd come to love about him, Rick met my eyes and said, "I do not believe you are the type of person to guarantee making an enemy when there is hope of making a friend."

Logan turned toward Polina, raised his coffee mug, and lowered his chin. In a serious, Rick-mocking voice, he said, "I do not believe you are the type of witch to turn down an invitation for beers and hot-tubbing when there's a perfectly good hot tub back at the motel."

Polina dropped her fork and started laughing.

"Just checking if bullshit works on all your kind or just her." He pointed his mug at me.

"Hey!" I said. "There's no need to be rude."

Rick glared at Logan.

"Oh, come on. This is not the time to needlessly defend your virtue, Grateful. We all know you're a good person, but this is life or death, sink or swim. You can't afford to be wrong about this. We need to get a witch in the bag, maybe two if someone doesn't step up." Logan pointed an eyebrow at Rick.

A growl emanated from Rick's chest, and the slightest bit of fang flashed between his lips.

I wagged a finger at Logan's face. "Said by the one person at this table who has nothing to lose if he goes home now! Back off. Rick's right. You catch more flies with honey than with vinegar. We try to win her over first. If she refuses, we knock her over the head and tie her up."

A waitress passed by our table at "tie her up" and scowled over her shoulder at us. She approached our waitress behind the counter and started whispering in her ear. I took a sip of my coffee.

Polina nodded her head and lowered her voice. "Sounds like we have plan B."

A few moments later, our waitress came by with a pot of coffee in one hand and our bill in the other. She was heavyset, in her fifties, and I got the definite impression that if any of us stepped out of line, the coffee pot would be used as a weapon. "You need more coffee, or are you ready for the bill?" she asked briskly.

Logan snatched the piece of paper from her hand, and she strolled away. "So, I guess this human with nothing to lose is good enough to pay the bill?"

"Logan…" I started. My mouth dropped open. What could I say? He was right. No matter how hard I tried to keep him out of danger, I always ended up luring him right back into it. We were using him, and I couldn't stop, no matter how wrong it was. I needed him.

"No, Grateful, I get it. Polina here has made it clear multiple times that I'm the lesser species to be used as you witches see fit. This isn't my first time on this merry-go-round. Tabetha broke me in, remember? I'll pay the bill, then I'll go back to my motel room and wait for my mother's ghost to tell me how to fix your boyfriend. Why? Because we're friends… Oh wait, friends are equals, aren't they? But then, it's just my life on the line." He slammed a few bills onto the table and stormed out the door.

Polina's eyes darted between Rick and me. "Was it something I said?"

CHAPTER 22
Valentine

"Logan!" I ran after him through the pebble parking lot and toward the motel, leaving Rick and Polina to sort out the bill. I caught up with him in the middle of the street and jogged to keep pace. "I'm sorry."

"You know, I thought I owed you this after everything that happened with Tabetha. You saved my life. I love you, Grateful."

That stopped me in my tracks. He stopped too and rolled his eyes. "Not like that. Not like you and Rick. Like family. I don't want anything to happen to you. I feel responsible for you."

"I feel that too. I didn't want this. I didn't want to put you at risk."

He took a deep breath. His hands found his hips and he gave me a short shrug. "Good. Then don't prolong this,

Grateful. Tonight, try it your way, but if this witch won't listen to reason, take her."

I stared at him for a beat, then nodded. "Understood."

"Come on," he said, motioning toward the motel with his head.

I glanced back at the restaurant. "Where are we going? I should probably wait for the others."

"No. We need to be alone. Every time my mother has helped me with something concerning you, we've been alone. The first time was in my apartment. The second, in your basement. During the whole thing with Tabetha? Not a word from her. I think Polina and Rick are messing with my reception."

I scrambled up the rickety metal stairs and followed him into his room. He closed and locked the door behind us, then pulled the drapes on the window. We stood in the dark for a second while he fidgeted with the brass lamp next to the bed. It glowed to dusty-ecru life beside us.

"What do you want me to do?"

"Have a seat on the bed."

I tipped my head to the side in question. Logan and I did have a romantic past, but I was not interested in going back there. I believed him when he said he didn't love me in that way, but still, he was a guy.

"Relax, Grateful," he said with annoyance. "Sit in the chair if you'd like. I simply need you to be quietly present while I do this. I think. I mean, I don't actually know, but it seems plausible."

I plunked down in the cracked vinyl chair in the corner. He took the bed, kicking off his shoes and sitting cross-legged on the mauve-and-mint comforter. He threaded his fingers together and rested his eyes on his clasped hands.

"What now?" I asked.

He shushed me. We sat in silence. I tapped my thumb on my thigh. Crossed my legs. Uncrossed them. Stretched my legs out and rolled my ankles. Cracked my neck. Tried to work out the words to an old song I liked in my head. Was it a diamond in the flame? A diamond in a flash? Something about bloodstains. Damn, I wish my phone wasn't dead. This was going to drive me crazy.

Are you okay? Rick's voice rang through my head, and I turned my face toward the door, mouth going slack.

I closed it before answering him in my head. *Fine. Trying something. Meet you back at the room.*

His footsteps passed the door, breaking the light through the crack underneath.

"It wasn't an angel," Logan said suddenly. Only his voice was an old woman's. His mother's. Logan was channeling his mother.

"What?" I looked back at him. His skin had gone pale, and his eyes were vacant like he wasn't even in his body. "Logan?"

"Your caretaker *is* missing his elemental magic, but it was not an angel who gave it to him, and it is not an angel who can heal him. Angels can't interfere. An angel did not help your caretaker," the woman's voice said through

Logan's lips. It was like watching a badly dubbed movie. At times Logan's mouth didn't seem to form the words fully, acting more as an amplifier than actually producing the sound. In fact, his entire form appeared stiff and catatonic.

My face tightened with concern for my friend, and I hastened to get what I needed quickly. "Then what or who was it?"

"I do not know."

"Bullshit. The creature who helped Rick was made of light! Where else but the beyond do things exist that are made of light?"

"If you swear at me, I will leave and never help you again, despite my son's affection for you."

"I'm sorry," I said. "Mrs. Valentine, please. I need your help. What could have finished the spell and given Rick his elemental power?"

"Apology accepted. Whatever it was, it was not from the beyond. If what you say is true, the light came from somewhere else. Light requires power. Follow the power. What power was there that day?"

I frowned. "Only *The Book of Flesh and Bone.* Reverend Monk bound me to my body with it. It cursed his parishioners and opened the hellmouth. But that book comes from darkness... the Devil. It was given to Reverend Monk by demons."

"A demon could appear as a reflection of light. Some are quite crafty."

Biting my lip, I shook my head. "It doesn't make any sense. Why would a demon give Rick power? I know what I saw. This creature helped Rick. I was dead. If it was a demon, why didn't he destroy Rick so I could never come back?"

"A smart witch might have predicted the attack."

"Right." I leaned back in my chair, thinking. I needed my grimoire or the copy of the spells I kept in a database on my phone, but *The Book of Light* was thousands of miles away, and my phone was both out of juice and dripping seawater. Still, there were a few things I remembered. "I readied the caretaker spell long before I used it. I might have had a booby trap to use a demon's power to my advantage."

"More plausible than an angel. One more thing," Mrs. Valentine said. Her voice had grown hoarse and soft. "Tell my son he'll soon be given a choice, and I…" Her voice faded away into oblivion.

Logan's body pitched forward, and he landed on his face on the bed. "Logan!" I rushed to his side and helped him roll onto his back. He moaned in pain as I straightened his stiff limbs. I slapped his cheek lightly. "Are you okay?"

"Nothing a shot of tequila won't cure," he said. "Did I pass out?"

"You just fell on your face."

"Damn, sorry it didn't work."

"But it did!" I said, surprised he had no memory of being possessed. Every other time he'd acted as a medium he'd relayed messages from his mother and was included in the conversation. "You channeled your mom!"

"Huh?"

"I could hear *her* voice coming out of your mouth," I said, poking him in the chest.

He rubbed the top of his head. "What did she say?"

I stepped over to the window and pulled back the drapes. It was raining again. Nice. "She said it wasn't an angel who gave Rick his elemental magic. She told me to follow the power."

"What power?"

"I think she meant the power that bound me. Reverend Monk used a book given to him by a demon to bind me to my body. He had to. I could have become a mist or transfigured into a bird and escaped being burned alive if he hadn't."

"Wait, can you do that? The mist thing?"

"Not now, but according to my grimoire I could at one time."

"Whoa."

I had so much to learn about being a witch. "The power of the book came from hell, which means it may have been a demon or the big bad himself who gave Rick his power."

Logan sat up, eyebrows knit. "Wait. Your job is to send evil supernatural beings back to hell. Your cemetery is basically a containment cell for escapees from hell. Why would a being from hell help you or Rick?"

I shrugged. "I have no idea. It's possible the demon did not intend to help Rick. I might have set a magical booby trap that drew on the demon's power without its knowledge. It's the only explanation. Hecate guards the door to the underworld. I help her do that. No one gets in or out without her permission. I can't fathom why a demon or the Devil would want to strengthen the gatekeepers."

"If it was a trap, how do we lure a demon into it again?"

I shook my head. "No idea. Replicated demon magic is well out of my realm of experience."

"Which means you can't fix Rick." Logan took unreasonable interest in his shoes.

"And we need to find two witches, not one. Rick won't work as the earth element in the spell."

"Fuck."

"I know." I looked at my watch, feeling overwhelmed. "Get some rest. It could get ugly tonight."

"Do or die," he said through a forced smile.

"You don't have to come," I said seriously. "In fact, now that we know about Rick, there's no reason for you to stay. You could go back."

He shook his head and laughed through his nose. "Shut up, Grateful. Go sleep. I'll be here when you wake up."

Mildly offended, I slipped out the door and made the short walk down the outdoor corridor to the room I shared with Rick. He was already in bed, eyes closed, although I could tell he was awake. The blankets were pulled halfway up his bare chest. As exhausted as I was, I yearned to explore everything under the covers.

"Then do it," he said before opening his eyes. He flashed a mischievous grin.

I blushed. "I'm exhausted, and I desperately need a shower." I tangled my fingers together in front of my hips. I needed to tell him he wouldn't work in the spell but was worried how he'd take the news.

"I know," he said, face falling. "Since we made love, I hear everything in your head."

"So, you know that I might not be able to restore your magic."

"And as a result there is likely no hope of restoring my memory." He cradled his head in the web of his fingers and stared at the ceiling.

I bit my lower lip. "I'm sorry." I searched our connection, but his feelings were a senseless jumble. I took a step toward the bed.

All at once, he sat up and tossed the covers back, revealing that he was, in fact, naked. My mind went blank, and all my blood rushed south.

"I don't need my memory to know that I want you," Rick said, approaching me with slow, even steps. "I don't need to remember how we got here for me to know that I made the journey. What we have is true." He reached out and cradled my face in his hands. "I don't need the past to know I want a future with you. I'm falling in love with you, Grateful, and it has nothing to do with who you were and everything to do with who we are."

Beguiled, I tried to reciprocate the sentiment but failed. All I could do was part my lips and give a sweet-Jesus-this-can't-be-happening sigh. His thumb caressed my bottom lip, his eyes fixed on my mouth. He was close enough for me to feel the heat from his body, and I became aware my chest was rising and falling faster than normal. "I love you," I finally said, breathless. "I've always loved you."

I fell into him, meeting his lips with my own. His weight pitched into me, and it was the most natural thing to let him back me against the wall, hard. His hand and my back took the brunt of the impact. I hitched one leg over his hip, and he ground into me, the length of him pressing into my jeans.

Rick grabbed my wrists and thrust my hands above my head. My shirt and bra were off and tossed to the floor in a heartbeat. His mouth trailed down my neck to worship one breast, and the backs of his knuckles grazed my belly on his way to the button of my jeans. I lowered my leg and shimmied my pants off, kicking them aside. I panted between kisses, my arms tangled around Rick's neck and head as if I could wrap myself completely around him. The need was undeniable. A hunger, an itch I had to scratch, had settled at my core and would not be denied.

Elbows braced on his shoulders, I wrapped one leg over his hip and climbed his body. He balanced my movement like it was choreographed, gripping me under the ass and entering me. Both feet off the floor and pressed into him in every possible way, my back hit the wall again as he began to thrust in earnest. I groaned, absorbing the impact with abandon.

A piece of drywall came free and fell across my shoulder. "Rick," I whispered. He didn't miss a beat. Pivoting, he carried me to the edge of the bed and lowered me to the mattress. He coaxed one of my legs to his shoulder and I gasped as he drove deeper. Arching my back, I supported myself on my elbows. He took the opportunity to graze my nipple with his teeth.

I came unglued, shattering around him and taking everything he had to give. When I came back to earth, I gathered my hair into one hand to expose my neck. I didn't have to coax him this time, or help him control the beast. He struck and he drank. The process was painless and required no help at all from me. When he was sated, he kissed me gently on the chin, the cheek, the eyelid.

"You should sleep," he said. "You'll need your strength."

"You're right," I said but held him to me when he tried to retreat. A slow, languid smile stretched across my face. "But first, a shower?"

"Allow me to assist," he said. He swept me into his arms and carried me to the bathroom.

CHAPTER 23
Pie

I was still sleeping off the effects of Rick's studious and methodical washing techniques when Poe and Hildegard returned with the news we'd been waiting for. The water witch lived in a log cabin along the river, and she was indeed new. Poe had seen her chopping wood the human way, presumably for a fire. He estimated her age in the early twenties, although it was hard to tell with witches. Magic kept us young. Even my half-sister Polina, who I estimated to be more than one hundred years old based on the age of the magic mirror she made for me, looked no more than twenty-five on her worst day. Still, I hoped the water witch was both young and inexperienced. We needed all the help we could get.

Once Julius was awake, we drove to a nearby patch of forest and climbed to the top of a hill overlooking the river. "Her name is Elana Woodsworth," Poe said.

"How'd you find that bit out?" Polina asked.

"Open mailbox," he said. "I wasn't going to get close to the woman while she was holding an ax."

I watched the curl of smoke rise into the night from her stone chimney. The rush of water down the river beyond acted as a reminder that although Elana was new, any witch was dangerous.

With his hands tucked in his back pockets, Logan asked, "What's the plan? Do we just knock on the door, or what?"

"Polina and I will go alone." I took Polina's hand. "We'll convince her that we're looking to form a coven, a support group for witches. I'm new and I reached out to Polina for mentorship, but we thought adding a third would be even better."

"You think she'll go for it? Witches strike me as keep-to-themselves types," Logan said.

I rubbed my chin and looked questioningly at Polina.

It was Rick who answered. "You should bring her something. Something to relax her to the idea." His voice was soft and confident, just for me. My own personal muse.

Julius seemed to sense our new connection and grimaced but agreed. "A spell to bind her, perhaps," he said with a hint of pain.

"A gift to open her mind to the possibilities." I plucked Tabetha's wand from its place next to Nightshade and with a quick flourish sent an intention into the ground. I was feeling strong thanks to my nap and my morning with Rick. From the point where my spell hit the earth, a bright green sprout shot from the dirt and climbed toward the moon. It branched and twisted, covering itself with leaves. Light swirled around the trunk and the shimmer of a spell colored the bark. The ends of the branches blossomed and faded, and then bulbous growths formed, growing ripe and heavy. An apple tree. The bright red fruit seemed to pulse with energy. I picked one and held it out between us. "Slightly intoxicating to lower her inhibitions," I murmured.

"Perfect," Polina said. "And something from me." She drew her wand and pointed it at a nearby stone. The rock shattered, and I shielded my eyes with my arm to protect myself from the debris. When the dust settled, a beautiful silver bowl sat in the stone's place. As thin as a spider's web, silver spirals bent into a hollow bowl perfect for the fruit I'd created. I pitched the apple into its center and picked a few more, each one more perfect than the one before.

"Come on." I picked up the bowl.

"Should we join you?" Poe asked, snuggled next to Hildegard on a branch of the apple tree.

"No. All of you stay here. If we run into trouble, I'll call Rick, and he'll tell you we need back up."

Julius flashed a bit of fang. "Of course. We wait for the gravedigger to tell us what to do."

"Not now, Julius," I snapped.

He hissed softly but backed off.

"You can do this, *mi cielo*," Rick said, and I felt like my heart might explode. *Mi cielo*, my sky. His name for me was back.

Logan crossed his arms. "Okay. Okay. Get going. We're here if you need us."

Bowl in hand, we descended to the small yard that surrounded the cabin and walked up to the door, the long, flowing shirt I'd worn billowing at the waist with my movement. Logan had been kind enough to buy Polina and me a few things from a local shop. We'd settled on modern witchy wear, bell-sleeved roomy tops over blue jeans. I liked it, but Polina missed her usual dresses.

When we reached the door, Polina knocked, and I cradled the bowl in front of me with a practiced smile. The door didn't open. Polina knocked again. Nothing.

"Elana?" I whispered.

The door creaked open to reveal a mousy young woman, all skin and bones and ashy brown hair. "Can I help you?"

Polina smiled sweetly. "No, but we can help you. We heard you were... new and came to offer our support and friendship."

I extended the bowl.

Elana sighed deeply and accepted my gift. "Come on in."

We entered a cozy room, *Little House on the Prairie* meets Frank Lloyd Wright. A fire blazed in the fireplace. Elana placed the bowl at the center of a large pine table and motioned for us to sit down. "I've had a feeling something was gonna happen all day."

"You did?"

"Yeah, a tightness in my stomach. I thought it might mean something bad was coming, but I think it meant you. I'm not good at interpreting witchy intuition yet. Like now, I sense magic in you; it's like the smell of strong perfume. But I can't tell anything more than that." She tucked a loose strand of hair behind one of her ears. "You must be used to that, but it's new to me. All of this is new to me."

"That's why we're here," I said, placing my hand on hers. "I've been a witch for less than a year. Polina's been my mentor and has made a world of difference to me. I told her I wanted to pay it forward and help someone else. When we heard about you, it just seemed like the right thing to do to reach out."

She filled her cheeks with air and blew it out. "You're relatively new also? It's overwhelming, isn't it? I mean, I almost drowned yesterday using my spell book to try to summon a piece of pie."

"Pie?" I looked at her questioningly.

"Yes, pie. I was sitting here alone, feeling sorry for myself for being called into this position, when it occurred to me, what good was having power if I couldn't do something useful with it? So I decided to conjure some pie. Well, I followed the spell in my grimoire to the letter, but no pie. The damn ocean poured out of the pages. It was all I could do to cast it back into the book before the water covered my head."

Polina laughed, then caught herself. "We've all been there."

"Sure," I said. "You don't have to do this alone. You can join our coven. We'll help you learn."

A small smile lifted the corners of Elana's mouth. "I'm so rude. Can I get you something to drink?"

"No," Polina said. "But if you have a knife, I'd love to split one of these with you." She pitched one of the apples into the air and caught it.

Elana nodded. "Sure do." She strode out of the room, into what I assumed was the kitchen, although I couldn't see it from where we were sitting. "Actually, I have something to ask you about already," she called to us. "If you're up for answering my questions."

"That's what we're here for," I called back. *Don't eat that*, I mouthed to Polina. She tilted her head as if to say, *I won't, duh.*

"I've had this dream the last couple of nights, and I can't figure out what it means. These silver people are shooting arrows at me. I try to fight them, but my power doesn't respond. It's horrifying."

"What kind of silver people?"

"Tall, pale people, with silver hair and pointy ears. I never know in my dream why they want me dead. They just do." She returned to the room with a cutting board and a chef's knife. "What do you think it means?"

I glanced at Polina. What did it mean? "Uh, hmm. Polina, maybe you should take this one." I selected an apple from the basket and handed it to Elana to slice.

"I don't think it's anything to worry about," she said. "Just your brain working out your new role."

She sliced into the fruit, the firm flesh parting with a snap. "I've been policing my ward, but I've never seen silver people like that before, not even in my human visions."

"You had visions when you were human?" I prompted, picking up a slice from the cutting board.

"All my life. Even before I was a witch, I could see the future. Well, sometimes." She picked up one of the slices and brought it to her lips, but paused before taking a bite. "Do you know what the silver creatures are called?" She bit, chewing the apple and swallowing.

"Goblins."

The wind picked up outside and rattled the windows. I turned toward the glass but could only see my reflection against the backdrop of night on the other side.

"I've never run into a goblin," Elana said. "Are they hard to sentence?"

"The hardest," Polina said, distracted by the same window I was. "They're fast and their blood is poison to witches. It's best to kill them from a distance if you can. I wouldn't even bother attempting to sentence one. Too dangerous to be that close. Of course, distance isn't safe either. They are excellent archers."

"I'll remember that if my vision becomes a reality. Thanks." She popped another slice of apple and hiccupped loudly. With a giggle, she placed a hand over her mouth. "Excuse me. Hiccups." She hiccupped again. "I should get some water."

She strode out of the room again.

"So, Elana," I called, "there is a spell that we developed to inaugurate new members into our coven. It's a simple spell meant to bind our friendship. Will you take part in it?"

"Of course! Do you want to do it here? I have a spell room in the basement."

A very wet basement surrounded by water, I thought. "It's kind of you to offer, but there's one more type of witch we want to invite before we do it. An earth witch."

"Oh, you mean Salome." Elana returned with a glass of water in her hand, hiccupping again despite it.

I shook my head. "Who's Salome?"

"The earth witch who was here yesterday. She's new too. Well, a couple of months. She came by to say hello and offer her protection. Put some wards around the house for me. It's how I knew I could trust you. You wouldn't have been able to step over the threshold if you meant me ill will. At least, that's how Salome told me it worked."

Alarmed, I turned toward Polina. Who was this witch? As much as I wanted to believe she had Elana's best interests at heart, I was skeptical. However, we needed her and her element. Perhaps Elana had a way to reach her.

"Did Salome give you a way to reach her? We could use her expertise in our coven."

"Hmm. She said she was staying with her friend at the lodge up river. She's originally from the East Coast. Rhode Island, I think. I could be wrong though. It's strange; her visit is a blur. I'd forgotten all about it until just now."

Until another witch messed with your brain and triggered a memory, I thought.

I stood up. "Understandable. You've had so much going on."

"Are you going?" she asked.

"We all are," I said. "Let's go find Salome and talk her into joining us. Then we can perform the bonding spell. I'm so excited about our new coven."

"Me too," she said. "Let me get my shoes." She left in the opposite direction as the kitchen.

Polina grabbed my arm roughly. "What are you thinking bringing her with us? You know as well as I do that this witch Salome is probably up to something."

"We can't leave her here. She could change her mind about joining us. We need to end this while she has the fruit in her system. If she comes with, we can perform the spell as soon as we take Salome down. I mean, if it comes to that."

"I hope you're right," she said.

Elana returned, Birkenstocks buckled onto her feet. "Everyone ready to go?"

We nodded and followed her to the door. She was so upbeat and trusting it almost made me tired. "You know, I have that feeling again in the pit of my stomach like something is about to happen. The same feeling I had before you came. Isn't that weird?"

"Yeah. Weird," I said.

Elana shrugged and opened the door.

There was a flash, and a silver arrow pierced her chest.

CHAPTER 24
Protective Instincts

"Elana!" I caught the witch before she hit the floor. Based on the position of the arrow, I prayed it had missed her heart, but her shallow breaths indicated it was implanted in her lung.

Metal pinged against metal as Polina shielded us from arrows with a stretch of iron she must have created from the country decor. "This isn't going to hold," she yelled.

With a puff of breath, I blew the door closed. The windows shattered, and we both hit the floor on either side of Elana.

"The arrow is poisoned with goblin blood. This could kill her, Grateful!" Polina yelled.

"Hold them back!" I said. "I'm a nurse."

She gave me a strange look, obviously questioning the relevance of my announcement, but did as I requested. Every piece of metal in the room melted and oozed into place to seal off the windows. The attack didn't ebb. Pings of metal on metal were joined by chopping at the walls and pounding on the doors. There were even footsteps on the roof, although I hoped the blazing fire in the hearth would keep those intruders at bay.

I tore Elana's shirt away from the wound. Black veins had formed around the entry point and spread from the source, her flesh ashen with the effects of the poison. I grabbed the shaft of the arrow, then retracted my hand when it burned my palm like acid. I wiped the goblin blood on my billowy shirt, then used the extra material to grab the arrow again and yank it out. There was blood and air and a weak scream from Elana. I tore off a section of my shirt and applied pressure to her wound.

"We need to get her to water so she can heal herself," I said.

"Downstairs." Polina scrambled to her feet and helped me lift Elana. We moved toward the back of the house, hoping the staircase was there. Elana couldn't help us. The poison had spread up her neck, and she was sputtering blood, her eyes glazed over. Polina tried a door in the wall. "Closet. Fuck!" she said. We continued down the hall.

"Do you hear that?" I asked, pausing.

"Hear what?"

"Exactly. The pounding has stopped. Do you think they gave up?"

"No way."

Grateful, help me shift. Rick's urgent plea came through our connection. Fuck, the goblins must have reached them. I closed my eyes and reached for his beast, tugging it forward until I could feel him complete the transition.

"Grateful! What the hell? Why did you stop?" Polina screamed.

I started toward the next door. We didn't make it. The rumble of a sliding mountain made us drop Elana. I'm not proud we dropped her, but with the house shaking and the thunder of sliding rocks, mud, and earth, there was nothing else we could do but hold on. The rumble and shake was a freight train, a jet taking off, loud and deep and coming for us.

"Avalanche!" I yelled.

Polina's eyes darted around the room. "We're in a wood house," she murmured. "Grateful, it's wood!"

With a flick of Tabetha's wand, I willed the logs to shift and close around us until we were housed inside a giant box. The protective response occurred just in time. We plunged into total darkness and screamed as the house slid away, us along for the ride. Locked inside, we tumbled, banging heads and being thrown into the walls as the house presumably came apart around us.

"If we roll into the river, we'll drown," Polina wailed.

I tried to steady myself on the wall, and my hand came away muddy. Concentrating, I strengthened and tightened the wood around us, willing it to branch and anchor us to the shore.

We came to a slow stop, but the slop of wet mud continued above us. I had to be careful not to light our shelter on fire, but I needed to see if Elana was okay. Softly, I blew into my hand and conjured a small flame to assess the damage.

Polina huddled in the corner, arms protectively covering her head, on the opposite side of Elana, who was now entirely gray. I reached for Elana's neck to check her pulse. When my fingers made contact, her flesh shattered and she disintegrated into a pile of ash near my toes.

I gulped a breath of air and shook Polina's shoulder. "Are you okay?"

She lowered her arms, and her eyes fluttered open. "What just happened, Grateful?"

Overwhelmed, all I could do was shake my head and look toward the ceiling that bowed and dripped mud. My mind fought what I knew was true. We'd been buried alive.

"No," Polina said softly, following my eyes. "The boys will come for us. They'll dig us out. Maybe you can make the wood grow. Roots part earth. I might be able to find metal in the mud. Elana… oh poor Elana."

I met her eyes. "The boys can't come for us. They're fighting the goblins. I helped Rick shift." I tapped my temple. "I can hear him in my head. The goblins are everywhere."

Polina sobbed and shook her head. "No… No… No…" She repeated the word softly, her pupils dilating with fear.

"Polina, breathe with me." I grabbed her arm and coaxed her through three deep breaths, trying not to worry about the amount of oxygen we had in this coffin of my creation. "We're safe for now. If we can last until Rick kills the goblins, he'll dig us out. It's going to be okay."

As if mocking me, the wood above us groaned. I tried to strengthen it with Tabetha's wand, but it wasn't enough. Section by section, the ceiling began to split.

"No, it's not. It's not going to be okay," Polina whimpered, shaking her head.

A splash of mud extinguished the fire in my palm, and with one last groan of effort, the wood around us gave way, and a wave of mud slammed into me.

* * * * *

I wish I could say that the impact of the mud knocked me out. It didn't. I experienced the crushing sensation fully conscious, the weight pressing all the air from my lungs and the grit of it denuding my exposed skin. Once the initial impact was over, the real horror began. I was alone. Out of breath. In total darkness. In pain. And I was dying. I could feel my light slowly extinguishing under the pressure of what I perceived as the hand of the goddess on my bones. She had squashed me like a bug, and now I would die.

It would not be an easy death. I succumbed to the temptation to breathe and sucked mud into my mouth. On the inside, the sickening snap of bones filled my head and my eyes... the pressure on my closed eyes was so intense I was sure they would pop. I was likely already blind.

I tried to go gracefully—to will my soul from my body—terribly regretful of my abandonment of Rick and the hard-fought love we shared. The dying part was taking much too long. The pain owned me. It tortured me, and I was helpless to resist.

Unable to breathe or barely think, I allowed myself to just... go.

I thought I was hallucinating when a hand wiped over my face and scooped the mud from my mouth. A breath of stale air pushed into my lungs. I couldn't see, but I felt myself sliding through a hole, my broken bones conforming to the tight surroundings in an unnatural and painful way.

Into fresh air, I emerged like a worm from the earth. The waft of breeze blowing over my raw flesh was both heaven and hell. I coughed and breathed and was fully aware that I was blind and as good as dead.

"You told me I cannot feed you my blood without your permission," Julius's voice said in my ear. "But your caretaker is not here, and I can feel you dying. Your soul slips from your body like the blood that pools around you. If you do not drink of me, you will die. Give me permission, Grateful. Trust me."

"Rick?" I asked. It was hardly a word. Just an exhale.

"He's shifted and is currently battling the goblins," Julius said. "He cannot come to you. The distraction of you could mean the end of all of us."

"No."

I felt him curl up next to me like a dog. "I will obey your wishes, Hecate, but it saddens me to watch you die. This long life will feel more like death without your soul in it. You have been a light for this ancient vampire." His breath was cold on my cheek.

My next breath rattled, and icy fingers tugged at my soul.

"Please. Your permission," he said. "You are very near death."

Again, I tried to die with dignity. I willed my soul out of my broken body, but it would not go. Deep inside, I wanted to live. I wanted to live so badly I was willing to cheat or lie or try anything, even the thing I desperately did not want to do but was my only hope.

"Yes," I rasped. "Permission."

The tearing of flesh preceded a rush of blood into my mouth. It did not taste like Rick's blood. It was not my personal ambrosia. Instead, it tasted like medicine, bitter and sour. It also worked like medicine. My eyes filled like balloons, and my vision came back in stages: light, objects, and then the crystal clear moon and stars above me. I swallowed again and felt my bones knit, my shoulders square. I could feel my legs again.

Julius moaned. "Finish it." He panted in my ear. By the pressure of his wrist in my mouth and the way he sweated and grimaced, I could tell this was not an enjoyable experience, but I needed more.

I swallowed again, and a severe itch crawled over my body. My skin felt too tight. In actuality, it was growing back, spreading over muscle and fascia. I was healing. After my last swallow, I knew I had to stop. Julius's blood tasted good, and an unusual and unexpected longing for him caused me to linger, licking the open wound on his wrist.

"Hold still," he said, and I did. I could not disobey. His words seeped under my skin like magic. It *was* magic. I'd bound myself to him.

I felt his lips on my neck and then a strike. It didn't hurt. In fact, it reminded me of Rick's bite, and I responded, stroking his hair and tracing around his ear. I lifted my hips against him.

He stopped abruptly and backed away from me like I had the plague. Licking his lips, he seemed almost in pain as he pointed toward the hill in the distance. "Go find your caretaker, witch."

I rose from the ground, thrumming with power. It was more than physical health. Having Julius's blood inside me was like being plugged into an eternal power source. I was one with the night, able to see in the darkness as if it were day. I was ancient and powerful. And I was going to find my caretaker and challenge my mother for her power. I felt along the base of my neck and grazed Nightshade's muddy hilt, thankful she was still with me.

Ready for war, I started in the direction Julius had pointed but paused and turned back to him when I remembered my friend. "Find Polina," I commanded.

He nodded and started to dig.

I turned back toward the hill where the cabin used to be and broke into a run.

CHAPTER 25
Fight or Flight

When I reached the top of the hill, I experienced Rick's beast in all its glory. The dragon-like creature was covered in silver blood, arrows protruding from its leathery wings and sides. I'd never seen so many goblins in one place. As many as Rick had killed, and judging by the silver pieces and limbs scattering the area around him it was quite a few, there were a hundred or more circling him. I shivered as I made out a barbed silver chain they'd thrown around his neck and were anchoring to the earth. I drew Nightshade, ready to do battle.

As I surveyed the combat from the cover of the tree line, I spotted two women overlooking the fray from a cliff of hardened earth that hadn't given way like the rest of the mountain. Without Julius's blood, I wouldn't have seen them in detail in the dark, but our new bond gave me access to his abilities. My borrowed vampire vision allowed me to zoom in, to see what my human eyes would not, from the distance. What I saw chilled me to the bone.

Bathory. I'd never forget the vampiress, from her voluptuous body to her wild black hair. She'd tried to cut out my heart once, to sacrifice me and kill my caretaker for a chance at a truly immortal, day-walking life. She'd failed and been captured and buried by Tabetha. But now she was free and apparently exacting her revenge on me and mine. Even more disturbing, she had help from a half-sister. The witch standing next to her was petite and Latina, with smooth dark brown hair tied into a low fold and large brown eyes that watched the battle below with an almost vacant expression. The earth witch Salome, I presumed.

Only because of Julius's blood could I make out the bite marks on the earth witch's neck. Certainly Julius wasn't the only vampire to know about the vampire/witch bond. Bathory was controlling this witch, and she had the goblins working for her too.

I didn't have time to analyze all the implications of this revelation. Rick was in danger, and I had no idea where Logan, Poe, or Hildegard had gone. Were they captured? Killed? I had a pretty good idea that Poe was alive. Our connection meant I'd know if he wasn't. But the others?

I drew my sword and charged into the fray. It was amazing to me how long it took for Bathory, Salome, and the goblins to notice me. The goblins were distracted with

Rick and certainly Bathory was as well, but a witch knows the presence of another witch. She feels it in her gut. In the past, Nightshade's magic had given me some amount of concealment from supernatural beings. That hadn't applied to witches before, at least Tabetha hadn't had any trouble sensing me. Perhaps Bathory's control had made Salome less perceptive. Whatever the reason, as I plowed into the goblins, sending heads flying in every direction, I had the element of surprise on my side.

Once again, Nightshade's blue glow fizzled as I attacked. Goblin blood neutralized my magic. It didn't matter. Julius's blood made me faster and stronger, like a vampire. I wielded Nightshade as I might a normal sword, and I aimed for their jugulars. Arrows flew in my direction. I dodged them, or I swatted them away with Nightshade's blade. One nicked my shoulder, but it didn't burn like before. Julius had said vampires were immune to goblin poison. Perhaps I'd been afforded some amount of immunity from ingesting his blood.

How long would it last? I didn't know, but I planned to use it while it did. I plowed through the goblins, rounded my sword, and sliced the chain from Rick's neck. Freed, the beast roared and attacked, scooping up goblins and crushing them between his teeth. He impaled more with his barbed tail and tore others apart with claws as sharp as scythes.

Just when I thought we had the advantage, Bathory yelled, "End her!"

The earth shook until I thought I might come apart at the seams. A schism erupted near my feet, and I shrieked as I tipped into the fiery split. But Rick was there, catching me in his talons and pumping his wings to fly me to safer ground. We landed across the chasm from the goblins just in time to see the earth witch topple over, despite Bathory's prodding.

Magic didn't come free. It wasn't endless. That's why the witch hadn't sensed me coming. Bathory had used her witch to exhaustion.

"Bathory, we have unfinished business!" I started up the hill toward her, Nightshade again glowing blue. A hand from behind stopped me in my tracks.

Julius. He'd arrived with Polina, both gritty and shredded. They looked like the walking dead, which in Julius's case wasn't far off.

"She's mine," he said to me.

"You again," she hissed.

"Me again." Julius bared his fangs. "How many times do I have to tell you, you can't have my coven, my territory, or my witch?"

Bathory laughed wickedly. "All of it is rightfully mine, Julius. Now, I'll have it back. All of it and more." Bathory leaped from the hillside and tackled Julius.

I dodged a silver arrow and bolted for Polina, who had taken shelter behind a spruce tree at the base of the hill.

"Are you okay?" I asked her, checking her over. She was bloody and damaged. One of her eyeballs was milky white and most of her skin was gone. Her arms hung unevenly, and her leg twisted to the side.

"Are you stupid? Of course not!" she snapped. "Never mind, I'm healing, but badly injured. It will take time. I cannot fight."

I parted the branches of the spruce. Rick's beast had taken to the sky and was attacking goblins in quick swoops to avoid their arrows, but he was growing tired. I could feel his power waning. Yes, he was immortal, but he could be imprisoned or injured beyond the loss of his memory. "Rick can't keep this up forever. What do I do? My magic won't work against them, and I can't kill them all."

"You must do the spell to challenge Hecate and you must do it now."

I spread my hands. "I can't! We don't have all the elements. Elana died. We don't even have a water witch!"

Polina grabbed my wrists. "Elana died at the hands of the witch at the top of that hill. That means Salome has access to the water element."

I shook my head. "When I killed Tabetha, I didn't have her power until I accepted her grimoire."

"Elemental power isn't created or destroyed; it just changes form. You had access to the power the moment you killed Tabetha. It would have stayed with you temporarily until another was called to rule her ward." She pointed to the witch passed out on the hill. "If Salome is still alive, she has earth and water, and you have wood and wind."

"And you have metal," I said, astounded. "We have them all."

She nodded, smiling weakly. "So, let's go."

"But I don't know the spell, and I don't have my grimoire!"

"There's no formal spell, Grateful, only transfer of power. I'll lend you my power, and you'll have to take hers."

"How do I do that?"

"You're wasting time. Come on." She grabbed my wrist and started limping for the hill, her right leg hanging as if it was disconnected from the joint. *Rick, I need you.* He broke from the goblins and landed clumsily by our side. I pushed her onto his back and climbed on behind her, plucking a silver arrow from his scales. They couldn't completely pierce his armor, but several were embedded, and he was exhausted.

"Almost there, darling. Get me to the witch."

With a rolling gallop, he took to the sky, landing next to Salome. The goblins shot at us, but the arrows couldn't make it across the chasm. They immediately organized, climbing down, searching for a way to bridge across.

Nearby, Julius and Bathory were a blur of thrashing claws and snapping teeth. Bathory was the older vampire, but judging by the crumpled witch before me, I was the stronger witch, and Julius was bonded to me.

"Here," Polina said frantically. "Draw the symbol."

"What symbol?"

"The symbol of Hecate. Quickly."

I used Nightshade to trace a circle, six feet in diameter, then copied the inner labyrinth I'd seen on the arrow fletching. The inner maze extended in three distinct sections, meeting at a wheel in the center. It was a rough approximation but I hoped accurate enough.

"What now?"

Polina stumbled into one of the three sections. "Put her in that one." She pointed at the other section.

I dragged the earth witch into the second section. She didn't fight me. She didn't rouse at all, though I sensed she was alive.

Polina took one of Salome's hands and one of mine. I took her other. "Try. Draw on my power."

I concentrated, feeling Polina's power leach into me, the taste of a copper penny permeating my mouth. When I tried to draw on the earth witch, I couldn't pull so much as a puff of dust. "It's not working. She's not awake to give me her elements." I stepped from my section and slapped the earth witch lightly on the cheek. Her eyes rolled back in her head.

"You'll have to kill her," Polina said.

"No." I shook my head. "I won't."

"Grateful, you have no choice. The goblins are coming. We have to do this now."

I looked over my shoulder. She was right. The goblins were forming a pyramid-style bridge with their bodies, hooking arms and legs to work their way across the chasm. It was a relatively slow process that involved a new goblin crawling across the heads of the first ones locked together and gripping the wall of the chasm. The bridge already reached almost halfway across. I could see a flash of platinum down the sloping terrain beyond.

"Kill her," Polina pleaded. "She's as good as dead anyway bonded to that thing." She pointed at Bathory, who had pinned Julius and was trying to rip off his head. "End this."

I looked from the goblins, to the earth witch, to the vampires. "I will end this."

I drew Nightshade and raced from the circle, straight to Julius's side. The distraction set Bathory off balance. Julius took the opportunity to flip her onto her back, and I didn't hesitate.

"You b—"

Bathory's curse was cut off as Nightshade sliced through her neck and her head bounced into the chasm. For a moment, I wondered if Julius would be angry at me, taking her life instead of giving him the pleasure, but he crawled off her body, jubilant.

"I need your help," I said.

"Your wish—"

"Compel that witch to lend me her elements."

"My pleasure." He rushed to the earth witch and shook her by the shoulders.

I followed, fully aware that the first goblin had stepped over the edge and the bridge was unmaking itself, the last goblin crawling across the others toward me.

"Now, Julius!"

"She has to look at me," he yelled.

Frantic, I slapped the witch harder without effect. A silver arrow passed between our heads—the advancing goblin shooting at us. "She needs strength. Feed her your blood."

He did. The blood rushed over her tongue, and her eyes fluttered open. "Lend Grateful your power," Julius commanded Salome. "You don't have much time, Grateful; this one is running on empty."

I took Salome's hand, thanking Julius as he left the symbol. With Polina's grasped in my other, I was helpless as an arrow cruised toward my head. Julius slapped it away.

"Remember our deal," he said softly.

"I promise." Polina's power came to me first, the copper penny, but as her hand linked with the earth witch's, more followed. A cool drink of water washed the penny away and the feel of cool earth under bare feet, wafted through me. The three of us started to glow, and then the wheel at the center of the symbol began to turn. The world spun, picking up speed until the light blurred and I could no longer make out either Salome or Polina.

I groaned as the spinning made my head ache like I was splitting in two, and then I saw myself standing across from me, and then another me, and another. Five versions of myself, one for each element. In the spinning circle, a pentagram of light formed, connecting each incarnation. As an arrow dissolved in the light behind my right shoulder, all that power plowed into me. I was no longer a point in the star. I was the star itself.

I pulsed with power and shattered into a million tiny pieces. When I came together again in the next breath, I was curled on my side on a soft bed of moss. I pushed myself up, rubbing my spinning head. I was in the jungle, beside a door inscribed with Hecate's symbol.

Only Mother wasn't here.

And the door was cracked open.

CHAPTER 26
Hide and Seek

I fumbled for Nightshade, but she was no longer on my back. Neither was the sheath I carried her in or Tabetha's wand. I'd been under the impression that if I united the elements, I'd become powerful and instantly be capable of fixing what was broken in my life. But instead of trumpeting into power, I'd been transported to Hecate's garden.

Then I remembered the last time I was here. Hecate had said if I found her and conquered her, I'd take her place. Was this part of the spell? Did I have to traverse the maze and challenge my mother for the power I needed to set things right? It seemed a contradictory course, but what other choice did I have? I was here, with no way back except through the labyrinth.

I approached the door, hands extended to my sides and torso lowered, ready for anything. At the threshold, I paused, searching the surrounding area for something I could use as a weapon. There was nothing. Not a rock or a fallen branch. I would have to do this on my own. With a hard swallow, I stepped through the stone door, scanning the labyrinth I'd been in once before for the threat of hellhounds. Dogs didn't attack me, but as soon as I was inside, the door slammed shut. I couldn't budge it on my strongest day.

The stone corridor I entered was edged with roots and vines, and fire burned in giant copper bowls every hundred feet or so. The floor was dirt and the ceiling stone, although the latter sloped on both sides, ending in a thin channel of exposed sky. That sliver of the heavens changed in a heartbeat, morphing from puffy-clouded blue to pitch black. Mother knew I was here, and she didn't like it.

"Which way?" I whispered, turning a circle. The corridor was identical in both directions. It was possible that Hecate's symbol was an accurate depiction of her home. If that was the case, it didn't matter which direction I went. Both led to the center, where I would find the goddess. If my intuition was to be trusted, however, this was going to be much harder than walking a maze. With a deep breath, I chose left, for no other reason than it had been the direction the hounds had come from the first time I was here.

I broke into a jog, anxious to reach the bend in the corridor, but once I was there, it simply curved again and again. I kept running. Minutes passed, maybe hours. Time had no meaning here, and every passageway looked the same. Was I going in circles? I paused. I needed a way to mark where I'd been or I couldn't be sure. Exhausted, I reached out and leaned a hand against a thick vine that climbed the wall. As soon as I made contact, it branched beneath my touch, growing and producing a series of bright orange blossoms. I retracted my hand. The blossoms stayed.

"Magic," I whispered, amazed at the stroke of luck. I might not have Nightshade, but I had power. The bloom was a product of the wood element within me. Could I wield all five? I turned to the nearest bowl of fire and released a short puff of air. The fire billowed. Air and wood were my intrinsic elements; what about my borrowed ones? Concentrating on the side of the copper bowl, I caused it to dip and scallop around the fire. Bingo. Next, I focused on the dirt and commanded it to pile into a small pyramid shape near my toes. Simple. I didn't see any water to use to test my mastery of that element, but certainly, I was not weaponless here. The natural power within me was still there.

I broke into a jog again, causing the vines on either side of me to bloom along the way. When I turned down one passageway and saw my trail of blossoms at the end, my fears were realized. I was going in circles. Turning back the way I'd come, I searched for an alternative course. No visible opening presented itself.

"Of course, it wouldn't be that easy," I murmured. "Time to use magic to battle magic." I placed my hands on the wall and closed my eyes. The stone was composed of metal and earth. I asked it for help, and it answered me. I slid my hand along the wall and was surprised when my fingers trailed into empty space. An alternate passageway, with an opening only as wide as my body, was concealed under a nest of vines. The vines parted at my touch, and I squeezed through into a darker, closer corridor.

Encouraged, I ran faster through this new section, my stomach clenching at the possibility that I was taking too long, that the goblins had overtaken my friends and Rick. I tried to focus, working my way through circles and dead ends. Thirsty and out of breath, I charged into a round room with a fountain at the center. I rushed to the water and cupped it in my hands to bring to my mouth.

The water touched my lips, but I didn't drink. Out of the corner of my eye, I saw my reflection in the pool. My hair was a tangled mess from being buried alive, and it reminded me of Medusa, which reminded me of mythology, which reminded me of the underworld. I let the precious water drain through my fingers and wiped my mouth with the back of my hand. I remembered something, vaguely, about not eating or drinking anything in the underworld or it would bind you to the place forever.

Crap! The thirst was incredible. My brain teased me with images of tall glasses of ice water, the impenetrable joy of the first sip. I forced a dry swallow and surveyed the room, anxious to get away from the temptation. There were five doors, each guarded by a stone statue of a hellhound. The five stone figures were gigantic, their shoulders as high as my head, and I breathed a sigh of relief that they weren't the growling, biting kind. I chose a door at random and tried to edge around one of the statues to get to it.

No dice.

Before I could reach the door, a loud crack of stone against stone pulled me up short. The statue exploded, showering stone fragments as I dove behind the fountain for protection.

A living, breathing beast leaped from the remains of the rock casing and attacked. Razor-sharp claws swooped toward my head. I ducked and ran beneath its stomach, trying to use its size against it. In the time it took to change course, I spotted a vine on the wall near the door and commanded the plant to circle the hound's neck. The beast kept coming, but the vine acted as a noose, tightening as it reached for me. Unfortunately, the vine was long enough for it to chase me to the opposite end of the room.

I pressed myself against the far wall, commanding the vine to retract. The heat of the hellhound's breath hit my cheek, its tongue extending as it hung itself in its quest to destroy me. I turned my face to the side, desperately commanding the vine to retract again. It worked. Inch by inch the hound receded. I breathed a sigh of relief too soon. The creature's left paw shot out and ripped across my chest.

"Ahh!" I screamed and clenched my jaw, flattening again against the wall. Slowly, mercifully, the beast wrenched backward, the vine dragging it up the wall next to its stone remains where it dangled helplessly.

I crossed the room to the door I'd so valiantly won only to find it locked. Pitching forward, I braced myself on my knees to catch my breath. The wound across my chest burned, I was so thirsty I couldn't think, and I desperately wanted to sit on the floor and cry. But I didn't. Instead, I forced myself to assess the situation.

Five doors. Five stone beasts. Why five? There were five elements. I surveyed the doors. This one had a vine—the only one with a vine in the entire room. There was one fountain, one bowl of fire, an earth floor, and of course, air. This was a test. I had to prove I was worthy of reaching Hecate, and only a witch who could wield all five elements was worthy.

With a deep breath, I gathered myself up and walked toward the next door to my right. As before, the stone cracked as I passed it, but this time I was ready. The beast erupted from the stone and barreled toward me, teeth thrashing. I faked sliding to the side and jumped instead. Whether by my own power or Julius's, I landed on the beast's back. The creature flopped and rolled. I leaped out of the way and did the only thing I could think to do. I blew. Wind picked up in the circular room, hurricane wind. I blew and blew, forcing the creature back until he slammed into the wall near his door. I didn't quit. I blew harder. The hellhound burst into flames.

Two down. Three to go.

Another door, another hellhound. The beast revived and charged. I reached out my hand, extinguished the fire in the copper bowl and re-formed it into a spear. Dodging claws and teeth, I slid in the dirt under the beast's belly like I was sliding into home on the softball field. In a plume of dust, I plunged the copper spear into the creature's heart. It curled in on itself and flopped off me, taking my spear with it.

My chest burned and bled as I negotiated the fountain to face the next one. This statue guarded a door mounded with dirt. Earth. I hadn't used that element yet, and I sent my power into the ground beneath my feet. The hound hatched from its shell and pounced. Retreating, I stomped, cracking a chasm in the earth beneath my feet. The gulch opened, swallowing the dog before it could reach me.

The last hellhound cracked its stone encasement. The only element left was water, which meant I'd have to use the element to kill it. Only, I hadn't manipulated water here yet. I'd left this element till last, because I was worried that Elana's power wasn't truly with me. The way I'd obtained it seemed shady at best. There was only one way to find out.

"Come out and play, little doggy," I said, beckoning it forward with my hand and circling to the other side of the fountain.

The beast leaped for me. With a grunt, I plowed my power into the pool, sending a geyser of water to intercept the beast and wash it into the fountain. Under the weight of my power, the beast drowned in less than six inches of water.

So much for self-doubt. I had them all, and I knew how to use them.

"Choose," my mother's voice boomed from above me.

"What? An element?"

There was no answer. There were five doors. Obviously, I had to choose one of them. But which? And what would be the consequences of my choice? I had to assume that the door I chose would deliver a challenge based on that element. Each of the elements was powerful. However, the element I felt most comfortable with was wind. It was my native element and the one I wanted to keep when this was all over. I decided I'd select wind first.

The deep wound in my chest throbbed, and I looked down at it in disgust. I needed rest and to heal. Rest was out of the question. Healing? I approached the fountain and washed out the bloody cuts, then cupped my hands and splashed some water over my sweat-and-dirt-caked neck.

"Choose!" The command came louder. With a groan of stone on metal, the room began to shift. The floor revolved, turning me within the doors. By the time I could react, the spinning threatened to knock me on my ass.

"Fuck!" I ran for the door with the burned remains of the hellhound next to it, but with the room rotating, I couldn't be sure if the door I chose was the one for wind or for metal—the bowl of fire had been directly in between the two. Hoping for the best, I jumped against the stone door. Thankfully, it gave under my weight. I landed on the other side, plunged into darkness. The door slammed and sealed behind me.

CHAPTER 27
Pop Quiz

"**D**amn. Learn a new trick," I whispered under my breath. My whisper bounced around the room, the hiss of it echoing back to me. It was too dark to see, so I blew into my hand, hoping my wind element would work here. A flame ignited in my palm. What I saw around me almost made me extinguish it. Snakes? No, some kind of worm. A long black specimen coiled down from the ceiling and latched onto my shoulder. I brushed it off, and it squirmed on the floor, contracting its sucker in a hungry pulse.

"Not worms. Leeches," I said in horror. I looked down at my bleeding chest and then up at the thousands of two- and three-foot-long leeches crawling toward me. I panicked. "Noooo!" I kicked them off my feet and stomped them under my heels. I brushed them from my skin and ran, sprinting through the corridor. They kept coming. Leeches poured from the walls, filling the room. So many that every time I lifted my boot, there was a suction sound as I tore them away from where they clung. I danced and squirmed, squealing when one landed on my head.

Still, I pushed forward until the black writhing creatures piled to my waist. I could feel them feeding on my flesh, boring under my shirt, wriggling within my clothing. The loss of blood made me weak, but that was the least of my problems. In minutes, I'd be buried in them.

"Think!" I told myself, my heart hammering in my chest.

And just like that, I remembered I was a witch. I blew, and the leeches burst into flames, but I didn't stop there. I blew and blew until the wind in the corridor was strong enough to tear everything in it apart but me. I blew and burned until my body ignited. I'd never been this hot, but the fire didn't hurt me. Within seconds, I'd incinerated the leeches to dust and cleared a path through the corridor.

"Fuck this place." Still flaming, I crossed the ash-filled passageway to another door. The bitter stench of burned leeches wafted after me as I exited into the next room.

As I crossed the threshold, the fire that had consumed my body extinguished. The door slammed, and I found myself in a hall of mirrors, naked. My clothes, I assumed, had burned away.

Frowning, I turned sideways and ran my fingers through my hair. I looked like hell warmed over. At least my reflection showed me one thing—my chest wound had healed. Great. Now I just had to process the inordinate size of my butt reflected in triplicate.

I walked forward, smack into a mirror. "Fuck. What's this fresh hell?" Trailing my fingers along the mirror, I tried to find my way out, but as far as I could tell, I was inside a box of silver. Silver. A test of metal.

"Honestly, you'd think this would get easier." Was I supposed to melt the silver? Cast myself into it? I placed my hands on the mirror and willed it to open for me. It obeyed, but I found myself in another octagonal room of glass. I was in a silver hive. I pushed and melted my way forward, until in my frustration, I accidentally broke a mirror.

"I sincerely hope that seven-years-of-bad-luck thing is just an expression," I said, stepping over the broken glass. I sighed. Another room. This was taking too long. There had to be a better way.

Closing my eyes, I concentrated, opening myself up to the magic in the room. A source of great power surged to my left. Unless I was grossly mistaken, that would be Mother. She was the only thing that made the hair on my arms stand on end. I turned in the direction, focused my power, and pushed. The mirrors shattered as if an invisible wrecking ball had plowed through them. Glass sprayed around me, the ringing cacophony causing me to cover my ears with my hands. When the pieces had settled to the floor, I cheered. A clear passage stretched before me, all the way to another door.

I picked my bare feet through the glass. It did not cut me. I took a deep breath before I opened the door. Surely it would lead to another test, but I wasn't sure which one. I told myself it didn't matter. I was ready for whatever Hecate threw my way.

Opening the door, there was no doubt which test I was entering. Water hovered at the threshold in a curtain, like I was looking down into a fish tank instead of vertically into a corridor. I wasn't an exceptionally strong swimmer, and the sight of a hammerhead shark swimming through the room did nothing to help my anxiety.

"Here goes nothing," I murmured. I poked my foot through the door. The water stayed where it was, hovering in the threshold. With one last deep breath, I stepped in, allowing the door to close behind me. Barefoot, I walked along the bottom of the sea, surrounded by razor-sharp coral and schools of colorful fish. None of the living creatures bothered me, but I couldn't hold my breath forever. In the distance, I could barely make out the door to the next challenge.

Lungs burning, I started to swim, willing myself to move faster toward the exit. The water pushed me forward at my will, faster and faster, but it was no use. The door seemed to be moving away from me at the same pace as I swam. Desperate for air, spots danced in my vision from lack of oxygen. I couldn't make it. My body wouldn't wait.

My lungs contracted, and I inhaled salt water. It washed inside, filling my lungs, and I breathed it out again. In and out. I settled into a rhythm, and that was how I discovered a water witch could breathe underwater. I remembered the bubble that had formed around Kendra. Apparently she hadn't needed it, except maybe to keep her dress dry. Laughing, I rode a tide of my creation all the way to the now stationary exit.

Almost disappointed to leave my undersea world, I pushed the door open and stepped out of the ocean. My foot landed on exotic green foliage. I coughed the water from my lungs, as the passageway closed behind me. This room was a jungle. The test of a wood witch. I ventured forward.

"Ouch!" I pulled my foot back and eyed the pathway. Thorns. The trail was covered in them. Now that I understood the tests, beating them was simple. With a wave of my hand, the thorns parted, as did the man-eating flowers and the strangler vines that crisscrossed the path. I reached the opposite door in record time.

"Earth," I said confidently. It was the only test left. I squared my shoulders and opened the last door. I was ready. At least, I thought I was.

CHAPTER 28
Bad News

I was wrong. I was not ready. Not even close. The floor gave out under me, and I tumbled into total darkness. "Ugh!" The air knocked out of my lungs as I landed on my back somewhere soft. Maybe a bed? I couldn't tell in the darkness. I tried to raise a hand to blow a flame so I could see, but my knuckles pounded against something hard and smooth. Carefully, I felt around me in the dark. There wasn't much room. I could only bring my hand to my face by first crossing my arms over my chest and then raising them to my chin. My wind element wouldn't work. I could not light a flame.

I'd have to explore by touch. I was in a crate. A small pillow cradled my head and hard walls surrounded me in all directions. I patted above me and to the sides, my palms slapping the satin lining of the crate. At first my brain wouldn't process where I was. It churned on the idea, searching for any other logical conclusion.

"Not a crate," I said. "A coffin." Judging by the element of this challenge, I was buried alive.

I should have remained calm. I had, after all, everything I needed to save myself. It wasn't enough. The memory of my time trapped in the mudslide came back to me. I was there again, crushed under a mountain of mud, skinless and blind. My heart pounded and I broke a sweat. I had to get out. I had to get out, NOW. I slapped the lid above, pounding on it with my fists.

"Help! Help!" I cried until I was hoarse. My hands bruised then bled, and tears streamed down my face. I kicked and scratched, my brain producing pictures of the miles of earth above me. No one could hear me scream. There was no Rick or Julius to rescue me. I gasped for breath, aware I was hyperventilating. Cupping my bloody palms over my face, I concentrated on slowing my breathing. "Just breathe," I told myself.

The rush of air through my nose and out my mouth helped me find my center. I was not helpless. The earth was mine to command. Slowly, deliberately, I willed the dirt to move from above me to below me. My elevation happened mere inches at a time. I don't know how long it took. It felt liked I'd been trapped in that box for days. Finally, light showed through a crack in the coffin lid. With one final push, I flipped the lid open and sat up.

So relieved was I to be free of the box, I climbed out onto my shaking and cramped limbs without assessing my surroundings. When I did, the gravestones lined up around me gave me pause. I could feel the dead calling to me under my bare feet. This was a cemetery, but not *my* cemetery. Not Monk's Hill. It was someone else's. Someone much more powerful.

The only door was one to a mausoleum, guarded by an ominous collection of gargoyles and hellhounds. It was cracked slightly, light as if from a flame filtering red and yellow through the opening. I stumbled forward, trembling. I wasn't cold; I was scared and exhausted. If my ordeal with the elements was the appetizer, facing Hecate herself would be my undoing.

I approached the door anyway, relieved when the statues stayed statues. With my last ounce of strength and courage, I pushed open the heavy stone door.

"Welcome, child," said an old woman's voice.

Confused, I passed into a cozy room with a fireplace, candles, and a braided rug. It was homey and welcoming. Hecate, in the image of the old crone, sat in a rocking chair in front of the fire, what looked like knitting in her hands. She smiled at me and put her work aside, pulling a jagged black dagger from her long skirts. I expected her to attack me with it, but she didn't.

Instead, she held the hilt of the blade out to me. Her smile was yellow and missing teeth. "Congratulations, Grateful Knight, you've passed the challenge. Now kill me and take your rightful place."

CHAPTER 29
The Old Lady

I'd never spoken to my mother in this form. I'd seen it those times when she'd appeared to me in all three versions of herself, but she'd always settled on the mother in the past. I'd heard it said the crone was her wisest incarnation, but also her most vulnerable. She hunched in her rocker in a black dress with a white lace collar, her fingers knotted and gnarled with age. She looked like a grandma, not a goddess. I struggled to wrap my head around the meaning of her words.

"Just like that? You're not going to fight me?"

The old woman laughed. "No, I'm not going to fight you. I'd help you if I could. Alas, if I stab myself with this thing, it will have no effect."

"What are you talking about?" Was this a trick? Was my mother taking this form to lure me to my doom?

Suspicious, I left three feet of space between us in case she lunged for me with the knife.

"You were always my favorite, Grateful," she said with a sigh. "No matter what name you went by, or what life you were living, you always chose love. Again and again. Lifetime after lifetime. Whatever temptations fate sent your way, you'd find that man or he'd find you."

"That man? You mean Rick, my caretaker?"

"Do you know how many caretakers there have been since the history of time?"

"No."

"Seven. Do you know how many remain?"

I shook my head.

"Five. Two found ways to break the spell after only a few hundred years. Thousands of witches. Thousands of my progeny with the potential to share their immortality—to love and be loved in return, and only five have successfully done so. And of those five, only one has died multiple times defending me and mine, and always comes back to her caretaker, no matter the difficulty. No matter the risk."

"What are you trying to say?"

"I have been the goddess Hecate for millennia." She raised her hand and gestured around the room. "Perhaps it is time I moved on. Who better than you to take my place?"

I shook my head. "I don't want to take your place. I never did. All I want is to live my life in your good graces, without an army of goblins trying to kill me."

"You don't still blame me for the goblins?" She laughed.

I bit my lip, remembering the two women I'd seen on the hill. Now that I was here, my mind finally processed the greater meaning of their presence. Hecate hadn't sent the goblins to kill me. "It was Bathory," I murmured.

"And Salome, the earth witch. The vampire Bathory convinced her that her ward wasn't safe after you killed Tabetha. Salome hired the goblins to kill you. Of course, she might have come to her senses had Bathory not bound her with her blood."

"No." My mind reeled. "If it was them from the beginning, why did you mark me?" I looked down at my chest. The scar she'd put there was gone.

"When I saw the way you stood up to me... the fire you had in you... I thought to myself, this is the one Hecate, this is the one to free us from an eternity in this labyrinth. She will be faithful, wise, and stern when duty calls for it."

"You bluffed to get me to unite the elements. You never intended to kill me," I mumbled.

She nodded her head slowly and smiled. "If I truly wanted you dead, I'd mark your forehead, not your heart. What type of idiot would mark your heart? Put on a shirt, the mark disappears. Thwarted again." She tossed up her hands and rolled her eyes. Grinning, she held out the blade to me. "The challenge is done. Get on with it."

"No." I took a step back.

"The time for choosing is over. The way back does not exist anymore, and the only way out is by killing me."

"I don't want to be a goddess. I just want my life back. What about Rick?"

Her hooded eyes widened. "What about Rick? Don't you see the gift I am giving you? Accept my role and you can cure him of Tabetha's mischief. He can be with you, here. He's immortal. He can exist here permanently."

"Here. In a stone labyrinth, cut off from our life? From the world?"

"It is the price a woman pays to become a goddess."

"No." I shook my head, starting to panic. I did not want to be a goddess. I certainly did not want to spend an eternity in a place like this. "No. I won't do it. I do not accept."

She tossed the knife gently in my direction. It clanked on the stone floor and skidded to a stop near my toes. She folded her fingers together and looked at me with the wisdom of a grandmother or a medicine woman, wisdom I could hardly fathom. "Then you will remain here, with me, for eternity."

"That's not fair. I didn't ask for this."

"Life isn't fair, Grateful. No one promised either of us fair. The universe does not require fair, only balance. Before you resign yourself to spending forever with me here, see what you leave behind." She stood and ambled toward the fire. With a wave of her hand, the flames danced and bent until an image of what was happening on earth came through on the vapors of heat.

I gasped as I saw Rick's beast chained to the mud. The goblins had overcome him, and his scaly skin bubbled as if his change back to human form was close at hand. I saw Polina, Salome, and my body still clutched to each other in the circle. The power of the spell glowed a faint blue around us.

"The goblins are unable to penetrate the spell, but your earthly power is fading. You are still human, after all. In time, they will kill you, and Rick will be alone. Salome will recover but your friend Polina will suffer greatly at the hands of the goblins—if they don't tear her apart and end her immortal existence first. Your familiar will die along with your human body, and your friend Logan…"

I turned my face from the fire to look at her.

"You don't know what became of Logan, do you?" she asked wickedly. "He tried to run when the goblins came, but poor, weak human that he is, he simply wasn't fast enough. They've captured him and hold him prisoner deep within the forest."

My heart ached with the knowledge she was telling the truth. "Is he still alive?"

"For now. Goblins have a preference for human flesh. They will keep him alive until their victory celebration. Then they will have him as a main course."

"No." I covered my mouth with my hands.

"It's your choice, Grateful. As the goddess, you could set all of this right. If you took the power from me, you could use it for the greater good. Who would be a more just and fair queen of the dead than you? You were born to do this. No one can do it but you." Half of the crone's crooked smile glowed in the firelight, the other half buried in shadow.

When I thought of my life's purpose, I always thought about my job as a nurse. For me, being there when a patient was at their sickest and caring for them when nobody else could was my purpose. I'd brought people back from the brink of death. That was my purpose. Not this. This was blackmail. I'd been tricked and manipulated.

I looked back at the fire and thought about Rick, suddenly aware again that I was naked. Would I have to spend eternity without pants? Maybe I deserved this. All my friends had helped me get here, and I had failed them.

"Why didn't you mention Julius?" I asked suddenly. "You showed me the fate of everyone but him."

The old woman shrugged and brought her fingers to her jaw. She turned from me, taking interest in the fire.

"What are you keeping from me? Julius's blood still courses through my veins and mine through his. He wouldn't just leave until I was dead." Could I even die? Or would I become some vampire/witch hybrid? He'd told me I couldn't become a vampire, but I could draw on his power. I shared all his abilities, so why did Hecate not want to discuss Julius or our bond?

With her back still to me, I picked up the obsidian blade. "It's time to end this," I said.

"That's right. Straight to the heart, dear." She pivoted and pulled her dress aside to expose the wrinkled skin over her chest.

The heart. Strange that to kill a goddess required the heart, which I considered the most human of anatomy. But then, she looked human in the light of the fire.

"Close your eyes. I can't do this with you staring at me," I said.

She gave a curt nod and did as I requested. I approached and pressed the tip of the blade into her chest. A tiny drop of her blood pooled against the tip.

"It must be hard to be a goddess. Lonely. Isolating. I can understand why you did what you did, luring me here."

She nodded her head and blinked slowly.

"You manipulated me, Mother, but I forgive you for it. I forgive you for everything."

A ghost of a smile flitted across her face.

"So, I hope you can forgive me for this." I sliced the blade against my forearm, quickly and silently, then pressed my blood to her lips. I wrapped my opposite arm around her head and pressed my wound into her mouth until I was sure she had swallowed some of my blood. Then I pushed her away.

"What are you doing?" she yelled, sounding younger than the old crone.

"I'm killing you." I brought the blade down, plunging it into her heart. I knew I'd hit my mark because the dagger jerked in my hand with each failing beat.

The crone toppled to the floor, the blade withdrawing from her falling body. I tossed the dagger aside and rolled her onto her back. I watched the light drain from her eyes as her blood pooled near my feet.

And that's when things got weird.

CHAPTER 30
Opa!

Pure unadulterated power forced my naked body into the center of the room. Once there, I burst into purple flame as if I was an elaborate dish a waiter had doused in brandy and ignited. As hot as the fire blazed, I did not burn. Instead, I expanded in the heat, growing until five rays of light shot out from my body. Each projection represented an element: blue for water, brown for earth, silver for metal, white for air, and green for wood. My purple fire burned down those rays of light and formed a circle around me. I became the cog in a mystical wheel, the five elements revolving around me, feeding me their power. I absorbed it all.

I lifted my hand in front of my face and watched it transform from the smooth skin of a young girl, to the muscular grip of a woman in her prime, to the spotted hand of an elderly crone. They were all different, yet all me. Time had folded in on itself. I'd become the goddess Hecate.

Soon, the room was too small for me. At my will, the walls of the labyrinth fell away, and I stood among the stars, the universe revolving around my hips. The heavens were still a mystery above me, but hell was peculiarly accessible. Tortured souls called to me from below my feet. I had too much going on to acknowledge their pleas. Unimaginable power poured into me, and my mind and my soul grappled with how to contain it, how to control it. The power consumed and confounded me. Past, present, and future converged. Was it today? Yesterday? A million years from now?

Becoming a goddess cannot be explained in human language. There are no words for the sensation of one's atoms exploding like supernovas or the intimate oneness that occurs with the life force of a single cell. The experience was overwhelming. So much so that I almost forgot what I'd planned to do with my new power. I'd become *this* for a reason.

The memory came to me on a warm breeze through the universe.

Love.

It would be romantic to say it was Rick who tethered me to reality. Our love was a strong and beautiful thing, certainly worth a stop on the road to immortality. But he was not the only checkpoint in my spiritual expansion. My sisterhood with Polina, the witch who had helped me get here at great personal sacrifice, also anchored me to the world, as did my friendship with Logan. Even Julius, whose bond had saved my life, and Poe, whose love mimicked a kick in the pants more frequently than a hug, crossed my mind, as did Michelle and my father.

I was loved, and I loved others.

In a state of infinite possibilities, it came down to this. All that mattered was love. Expanding further, moving beyond the plane I was in, took me farther away from love. And so, as painful as it was to do so, I stopped becoming the goddess and turned away from the increasing power.

I had promises to keep.

With everything I had, I concentrated on returning to the ones I loved. To do so, I had to contract and stretch the tethers that bound me to the wheel in the labyrinth. I was relieved when the magic obeyed. I arrived in the forest outside the goblin battle. Not exactly where I'd expected to be. I'd focused on Rick, but defiantly my magic brought me here.

Ahhh! Logan's screams drew my attention and I walked to a clearing nearby. He was bound to an oak tree, two platinum-headed goblins poking him with daggers and drinking his blood.

"Leave him!" I said, but the words came out jumbled, like I was speaking in a different language.

The silver heads turned to face me. "Who are you?" the female asked, drawing her bow and pointing a silver arrow in my direction. I recognized her, although her existence seemed insignificant now.

The male she was with pointed his dagger at me. He couldn't operate a bow because he was missing a hand.

"Tobias," I said and took a step toward him.

The female wrinkled her nose and released the arrow. It hit me squarely in the stomach. I laughed at the faint tickle of silver before my power melted and absorbed it.

With a deep breath, I sent a gust of wind in their direction, careful to avoid Logan. The goblins shrieked and blew apart piece by piece, raining silver chunks at Logan's feet.

Logan's heart fluttered in panic. I could hear it like the beat of hummingbird wings inside his chest. He kicked and pressed himself against the tree to escape me.

"Relax," I said softly, although it was clear he didn't understand me. I waved a hand and the branch of the tree reached down and broke the silver chains binding him.

He shielded his eyes and looked in my direction. "Grateful? Is that you?"

"Yes," I said, but he shook his head. He didn't understand me.

Poe and Hildegard landed in a branch of the tree. "Thank you, my queen," Poe said reverently.

I bowed my head slightly in acknowledgment as a cry of pain rang out from the hillside. With one look back at Logan and Poe, I changed course. With some effort, I concentrated on Rick and transported myself to his side. On the edge of the battlefield, he'd succumbed to his human form again and was naked and shivering under a crisscross of goblin chains that sizzled against his flesh.

Julius, pale and bleeding, frantically fought the goblins, his efforts to protect my lifeless body increasingly less effective. The goblins were winning. Time to turn the tables.

Stretching my arms to my sides, I focused all my anger on the goblin army. I didn't simply draw on one element, but all of them. I released a blast of energy embodying all my hatred for their kind.

I'd never really understood that word *smote*. Like in the biblical sense... *the angel of the lord smote him*. By context, I could have guessed it was bad, but not until this moment on the mountain did I actually get it. I smote the goblins. I didn't just kill them. All that was left of an entire legion were a few smoking silver parts. The rest? Obliterated, their shadows burned into the hillside.

Julius recoiled at the destruction, then scrambled to face me, falling on his knees and bowing. I almost laughed at his reaction, but I realized I must not look like me, considering my body was still here, huddled in the circle.

"You are free," I said to him in my jumbled language. I clipped the metaphysical string I could see holding him to me, well, to my human form.

He jerked as if a giant weight had been lifted from his shoulders, but he stayed where he was.

My human body, now safe from goblin harm, huddled within a dying spell, pitched forward in the web of Polina and Salome's arms. We were holding each other up by force of will, but we wouldn't last forever. I was on borrowed time, and there were things I needed to do.

My attention turned to my caretaker. With a blink of my eye, the chains binding him dissolved and blew away. He didn't get up. Probably couldn't. He rolled his head to look at me, and his eyes widened in the glow of what I'd become. I was ready to give him what Tabetha had taken: his memories and his element.

But as I approached, I saw myself reflected in his eyes. I flickered in his pupils like a candle flame. The image I saw was humanoid and made of light, with tendrils of power trailing behind her like wings. I looked like an angel. I was made of light.

The memory of Monk's Hill, when Polina had showed me Rick's transformation, flashed through my mind. It all made sense. It wasn't an angel who had given Rick his magical element; it was me. And in order to replace what Rick had lost, I had to go back to the time and place of its loss.

But first, I wanted him to know who I was. I lowered my lips to Rick's ear and gave him our history with one word. "Remember." His eyes fluttered against my light, and I cupped his cheek in my hand.

Concentrating on 1698, on the moment I'd seen the angel complete Rick's spell, I left him on the hillside of Mount Coffin and passed through time and space to the day of my first death. I funneled down from the sky, eyeing my burned and crispy corpse bound to the stake in front of Monk's Hill Chapel with an odd detachment. I willed the fire underneath her to extinguish.

Rick's prone body shivered in the dirt at the base of the hill, and I rushed to his side. It took effort to hold myself here. I felt stretched, like I was tethered to the labyrinth by an elastic band that was being twisted, drawing me back.

Rick blinked at me, his mind unable to absorb who I was or what I was. Cupping his face in my hands, I could see my mistake. When Isabella, my first incarnation, had completed the caretaker spell, she had failed to provide Rick with a mentor. His element was there, buried deep inside, a product of the caretaker spell, but he had no one to draw it out. There were so few caretakers, after all. She might have done it herself had she lived long enough, but instead she left it to me, the future version of herself.

Tabetha's spell, the persigranate she'd forced on Rick, had targeted me. She'd ordered him to forget me, but I was part of the spell that had made him a caretaker. When he forgot me, he also forgot how to access his power. *I* had completed the spell, not in 1698, but today, when I'd traveled back in time to bestow a final gift on him.

"Become," I said. The word came out jumbled as before, but he understood. His eyes widened, and a current of energy flowed between us. In that tether of energy, I coaxed the earth element from his heart. "Become," I said again, more softly.

"I will," he said.

I pressed a kiss to his lips. It was necessarily short. The gravitational pull the universe had on me was too strong to deny any longer. Arms outstretched, I returned the way I'd come, in a column of light.

* * * * *

With a painful jolt, I arrived in the labyrinth at the exact moment I'd stabbed Hecate. It took concentration to fix myself firmly in that place and time. At the center of the wheel of elements, I worked again to contain myself to fit inside the room. The stone walls seemed suffocating after my journey through time and space.

What I was about to try was dangerous. If I survived, I wasn't sure what life might be like. Would I still have my mind? Would I ever see the people I loved again?

I turned in the direction of the metal element and focused all my intentions on Polina. "Return," I whispered, and I cut the silver ray of light between it and me. I repeated the incantation with earth, focusing on Salome. "Return," I said again. The brown element didn't leave me exactly, but I could feel it split and dull. When I got to wood and water, I focused on the old crone lying dead on the floor near my feet. "Return," I said. The blue and green elements broke off from me and floated into the old woman's body.

Wind I kept for myself.

When I was done with this process, I pulled the wheel inside, grunting with the effort and used all my magic to extinguish the purple flame. I knelt beside the old crone. She wasn't breathing, but that was what I expected. She had to die for me to take her role, even temporarily.

I tipped her head back and started CPR. Two big breaths, then thirty chest compressions. I counted in my head *1 and 2 and 3…* I'd given her vampire blood— Julius's blood in mine. If my theory was correct, it would heal her torn heart. All I had to do was get it to beat again. If I could bring her back, there was a chance it would reverse the spell and return Hecate's power to the proper place.

I continued CPR, focusing my intention, my power, on healing the wound I'd caused. I was the goddess, but I couldn't raise the dead. Still, when the crone had told me I needed to stab her in the heart, I realized that when I became the goddess, she would become human. Human hearts could heal. Human hearts could stop and be made to beat again.

Gasp! Hecate opened her eyes, and the breath of life filled her lungs. With her inhale, each of the five elements plucked from my chest and floated into her gaping maw. Earth, metal, wood, water, and even wind, although I felt a portion of the last stick to my insides like a coating of tar.

By her second breath, the room didn't feel claustrophobic anymore, but then, I was small again, human and witch. I waited, wondering if my minutes were numbered. Would she destroy me for my insolence? Keep me prisoner here for eternity?

It didn't matter. I had done what I was supposed to do. I believed with my whole heart I'd done the right thing.

The old crone rose from the floor without any deference for gravity. She did not bend or use her knees. She floated from lying to standing in one unnatural and horrific movement. The vibration was back, her three forms shifting, fighting for control. The crone was still there, as was the mother, but this time Hecate settled on the maiden.

Her wide-eyed innocence took me aback. She looked young, maybe seventeen, with a dark braid over one shoulder, and a sheath dress that accentuated her smooth skin and straight spine.

"You didn't follow through," she said through full red lips.

"I couldn't. I never wanted the power, just to make things right again. I won't become the goddess. I won't take your immortality. I don't want it."

"Am I to understand you sacrificed yourself and denied the lure of power to save the people you loved?"

"Yes. That's right. This existence isn't for me."

"Yet, here you are." She folded her hands in front of her.

"You can keep me here until my body dies, I suppose." I frowned. "Maybe forever. I don't actually know how souls work. But if you do, I don't think it will get you what you want."

"No? Tell me, Grateful Knight, what it is you believe I want."

"You want a friend, a sister, and a daughter. You want someone to care for you and to understand that tiny bit of you that remembers being human."

She batted her long eyelashes at me. "An interesting hypothesis."

"I'm pretty sure death isn't the answer, even for a goddess."

"You were always my favorite, Grateful Knight." Her form shifted again from the maiden into the confident middle-aged woman I called the mother. "I have tested you, and you have failed."

I stiffened. "What are the consequences of failing?

She grinned and in the next moment we were in the jungle outside her labyrinth. I was still naked, and I hugged myself in the chilly climate. "Your consequence is that you go back where you came from."

I breathed a shaky exhale of relief.

"And Grateful, keep to one element from now on."

"Of course."

She placed her hands on my shoulders and flooded me with warmth, and then leaned forward to kiss me on the cheek. In the blink of an eye, I was flat on my back on the hillside in Washington, clothed in the torn, gritty rags I'd been wearing during the spell, and staring up at five extremely concerned faces.

Polina and Salome gasped in witchy unison and looked at each other as if they'd just witnessed a miracle.

"What?" I asked.

"You were dead," they said together.

I laughed. "I wasn't dead." I made it sound like the mere thought was ridiculous.

Logan raised his eyebrows. "Damn, you are hard to kill."

"The hardest." I pushed myself to a seated position.

Julius offered me his hand. "Not just hard to kill. As good dead as alive."

"You stayed," I said to the vampire, allowing him to help me up. "I broke the bond. You don't have to help me anymore."

"You did, and I don't," he admitted. "I stayed... for political reasons."

"Thank you," I said softly.

He looked away.

And finally, there was Rick.

My caretaker opened his arms, and I stepped into his embrace. He kissed my forehead, my cheek, my hair. "Take of me," he said, offering his throat.

I pulled back slightly. "Rick, do you remember? Us from before?"

The corner of his mouth lifted slightly, and his eyes crinkled at the corners. "Everything, *mi cielo*. You are my sky, my beginning and my end."

I blinked back tears as he lowered his lips to mine.

CHAPTER 31
Full Circle

Salome took her leave of us on the hillside, anxious to get back to the life she'd neglected under Bathory's compulsion. Her previous concerns about me seemed moot now that I no longer housed Tabetha's element. I wasn't sure who would take over as Salem's witch, but we both agreed to help whoever Mother called to the task. I didn't fully trust Salome and never would, but I gave her the benefit of the doubt that her choices concerning the goblins were made under Bathory's control.

The rest of us returned to the hotel to pack our things.

Later, in her room, I confronted my half-sister for her selfless involvement. "I owe you one," I said to Polina.

She snorted. "You owe me a hell of a lot more than one." She pointed at her milky eye.

"Yes, I do," I said seriously. "Anything. Anytime."

A single tear pooled in the corner of her lower lid, and I pulled her into a tight hug.

"We're driving the hearse back to New Hampshire. We could take a detour and drop you off in Smuggler's Notch if you want."

She shook her head. "No offense, but I'm not up for a long car ride. A little gold dust and Hildie and I will be home within the hour." She patted the bag on her hip.

I kissed her on the cheek. "I'll phone you when I'm back home."

She smiled. With a whistle around her thumb and middle finger, she called Hildegard. The snowy white owl barreled through the open window and landed on her shoulder. A blur of black feathers wasn't far behind. Poe. My raven landed on my outstretched arm, dejected.

"I'll miss you, Hildie, my darling. Remember, I am only a night's flight away," Poe said. His voice cracked with emotion. I raised an eyebrow. My smart aleck, pain-in-the-ass familiar had an honest-to-goodness crush.

For her part, Hildegard squawked her goodbye as owl and owner stepped into the tiny bathroom. With one last wave through the door, there was a flash of gold, a flush of water, and they were gone.

"I don't think I'll ever get used to that," I said to Poe. "I mean, the germs alone." I shook my head.

Poe sniffled. "The gold dust? At least she's not stuck riding in a hearse across the country with a wind witch who can't fly." He rolled his eyes.

I lowered my arm, sending him flapping to the dresser. "A wind witch who can't fly," I mimicked through a grimace and flipped him the finger. *Asshole.*

There was a knock at the door, and I crossed to open it. Logan.

"We're all packed. The sun is rising so Julius is already locked in the coffin. Rick's got your stuff loaded. I can take the first shift if you want," Logan said.

He scratched the scruffy beard that had formed over the length of our journey while he waited for an answer. I took two steps, threw my arms around him, and kissed him squarely on the cheek.

"What was that for?"

"For abandoning your business, spending your money, and risking your life… for me. Thank you, Logan. I owe you one."

He snorted. "You owe me a hell of a lot more than one!"

I laughed. "You know, Polina said the exact same thing."

"Hmm. Maybe that redhead has a brain in her skull after all."

"Logan, are you blushing? Do you have a crush on Polina?"

He shook his head vehemently. "You're a great friend, Grateful, but your kind are crazy-ass bitches."

"Understandable."

I cast a sharp glance back at Poe, still smarting from his comment. "Shall we go?" My familiar soared out the door between us.

We made our way to the hearse where Rick was waiting, leaning against the dusty black metal with his arms crossed over his chest. He smiled when he saw me, and I hurried to his side.

"What are you grinning about?" I asked, kissing him firmly on the lips.

"I find it humorous that I loved you even before I remembered you."

"What made you think of that?"

He unfolded his arms and held out his right fist, then slowly unraveled his fingers.

"My ring!" The platinum setting with it's blue cushion of gemstones winked in the sunlight.

"I noticed it in the silver pan when we were escaping Julius's safe house. I remembered it on your finger, and I took it with me."

"And you didn't think to give it back to me until now?"

"Oh, I thought about it quite a lot. But when I gave it back to you, I wanted it to mean something. Like now."

Rick lowered himself to one knee in front of me. "Grateful Knight, will you marry me, again?"

I held out my hand and allowed him to slide the antique ring onto my finger where it belonged. "You'd better believe it. Only, this time, I'm not leaving anything to chance."

"No?" He grinned, still holding my hand.

"No. When we get home, you're moving in with me, and I'm not letting you out of my sight. Not for a very long time."

He stood, grinning from ear to ear. "You're not worried about my earth element tempering your magic?"

It was an old excuse. One I'd used over multiple lifetimes. If it were true, it was only mildly so. However, I was pretty sure it was just something I'd said, a way to preserve a last bit of independence, to not give myself fully to him. I was done with considering past reservations. I loved him with my whole heart, soul, and mind, and I would be with him.

"Not worried at all," I said.

He swept me up in his arms and spun me around to Poe's cheers and Logan's slow applause. Then we climbed into the hearse, and we headed for home.

* * * * *

"So, you actually became a goddess?" Michelle peered skeptically over her coffee at me.

"I did. I smote an entire legion of goblins with a flick of my finger." It was actually a pulse of my open arms, but, hey, my story to tell.

"And you turned all that down for Red Grove, New Hampshire?"

I took a sip of my cappuccino and glanced toward the door of Valentine's. It was early morning on a sunny day—a gorgeous day full of hope and potential. "Let me put it this way. Imagine that NASA tapped you on the shoulder and asked you if you'd like to be the next astronaut to go into space."

"Hell yeah!" Michelle said, pumping her arms above her head.

"Wait. There's a catch. It's a one-way ticket. You have to say goodbye to everyone you've ever loved. Manny, the baby, all your friends. You will be in a suspended state for eternity, while each of them lives out their lives and dies back here. Would you do it?"

"Of course not," Michelle said. "But that's not how it would have been. If you were a goddess you could've gone wherever you wanted. You could've visited. And Rick's an immortal. You could've been with him forever."

I shook my head. "No. It's hard to explain, but I wouldn't have been me anymore. I wouldn't have had a life; I'd have an existence. I didn't want that."

"What was it like?"

I chewed my lip trying to think of ways to explain it. "It was like the first time you ever saw the ocean, times a billion."

She stared at me until the silence was awkward. "Now that you're human again, how's the living together business going?"

"Perfect. Not that different actually. I'm looking forward to the marriage business."

"Have you set the date?"

"Noon on July 21—the summer solstice. Can you wear the bridesmaid's dress one more time?"

"Are you kidding? I live for that shit, but I thought you wanted to be married on the spring equinox, because of its association with new beginnings."

"Yeah, funny thing, I hadn't realized that my element, air, was also called wind or fire, depending on what culture you're from. Turns out it is highly associated with summer. So, the summer solstice brings renewal for me. Isn't that weird?"

"It's in less than a month."

I shrugged. "These things practically organize themselves."

"When you can wave your magic wand."

"It does have its perks."

Michelle leaned back in the booth and looked at her watch solemnly. "I gotta go. Shift starts in ten."

"Say hi to everyone for me." I tried not to look too disappointed not to be going to work with her.

She stood and rounded the table to give me a hug. "I love you, Grateful. I'm glad you didn't leave us for infinite power and immortality."

"Me too."

* * * * *

We didn't bother with invitations. We called the people who mattered and told them about our short-order wedding. They lined the pews, smiling at me as I waited at the back of the church. Logan, Michelle's family, the nurses I used to work with, townsfolk from Red Grove who Rick had formed relationships with over the years, and even Poe and Hildegard, who sat inconspicuously in an open window, waited for Rick and me to make it official. It was a small group but an important one—all we needed to help us welcome in our new marriage.

"It's time," my father whispered in my ear. I hadn't even noticed that the pianist had begun my processional. I was distracted by the man at the end of the aisle who was obviously distracted with me. Rick.

Step by painfully slow step, I made my way to him. My father kissed me and a rush of surety came over me. I was certain down to my soul this was where I belonged. I had loved Rick from the beginning, maybe from the first moment we saw each other, and I would love him forever and the forever after that.

The pastor began the ceremony and this time, nothing stopped us from saying our vows.

"Grateful,

Today, I take you as my wife, to love in this life and the next.

A single lifetime is a cup too shallow to hold the abundance of my love for you.

I bind myself to you today and always,

And will never leave or forsake you from this day forth."

He slid the blue diamond ring I'd worn on my right hand onto my left.

"Enrique Ordenez,
Today, I take you as my husband,
As my beginning and my end.
I bind myself to you, heart, mind, and soul.
I will walk by your side until the mountains crumble and the seas turn to dust.
And will be true to you until death takes me."

I slid a thick platinum band on his finger. At that moment, he was my entire universe. I didn't hear how the pastor finished the ceremony, hardly noticed the applause, but when Rick kissed me, there was no doubt that our marriage went far beyond this world. We were bound, connected permanently, our lives and hearts interwoven.

When we finally pulled apart, for a moment, just a fraction of a second, I thought I saw my mother, Hecate. At the back of the church, she smiled at me, her hand over her heart in silent blessing. And then she was gone.

* * * * *

After the ceremony, we gathered at the Gilded Rooster, which was the only reception hall available on short notice. Logan had offered to bump the couple who had booked Valentine's, but it seemed a cruel thing to do to someone. I'd declined his offer to his obvious relief.

We dined on rubbery chicken, fed each other dry chocolate cake, and laughed with our guests as the wine flowed. We kissed when bored attendees clinked their glasses with their forks. And just after sunset, a buck-toothed boy with a bad haircut announced the first dance of Rick and Grateful Knight. He'd decided to take my name, a final way of joining me in this time, in this life. It made me feel like I was his and he was mine.

The music changed and my father cut in for the father-daughter dance. "I think your mother would be proud," he said. He meant my biological mother, but the comment made me think of Hecate.

"Yeah, I think you're right."

"I'm proud too."

I laughed. "You're proud that your daughter is an out-of-work witch?"

He shook his head. "I'm proud that my daughter is a good person who knows how to love someone."

"Oh, Dad," I said, pulling him into a hug. "I love you."

"I love you too. Now, is it too early to talk about grandchildren?"

I rolled my eyes and slapped him on the shoulder. "Only if you want to keep talking."

The song ended, and I searched the room for Rick. My gaze caught on a figure waiting in the shadows just inside the sliding glass door that led to the patio. Julius.

"Excuse me, Dad." I squeezed his hand. "I see an old friend and want to say hello."

"Go ahead." He kissed me on the cheek and returned to his table.

I crossed through the other guests and greeted the vampire.

"Congratulations, Mrs. Knight." Julius flashed a little fang and bowed at the waist.

"Thanks. You know, if you keep acting like a friend to me, I might suspect our bond is still intact."

He shook his head. "No. I assure you I am free and exercising that freedom quite regularly." He touched the tip of his fang with his tongue and leaned his back against the wall. "Grateful, there are few people in this existence I can call friends. Would I be wrong to think you are one of them?"

I theatrically swayed my head back and forth on my shoulders. "No. Not wrong. We're friends."

"Good, because I have a wedding gift for you." He handed me a business-sized envelope.

I ripped into it and unfolded a letter. "It's from the Human Resources manager at St. John's. They are reinstating me at the hospital and apologize for the misunderstanding." I held out the paper and stared at him with wide eyes. "You got me my job back."

"A few... conversations and they couldn't refuse. They need you there, after all. Not enough good nurses these days. Even fewer who can treat the supernatural population in Carlton City."

In shock, I reread the letter several times. It was real. I was a nurse again. A rush of joy overtook me, and I tossed my arms around Julius, pressing my lips to his cheek.

"Thank you," I said, pulling away.

He shrugged, but a hint of a smile turned his mouth.

"I think they have scotch at the bar," I said, pointing a thumb behind me.

A human waitress in a short gingham dress passed behind me with a tray of empty glasses. He inhaled deeply. "I love barbeque, don't you?"

"Not without her consent," I whispered, but judging by the look-over the waitress gave Julius as he left my side, I didn't think he'd have a problem.

I searched the room for Michelle, holding up the letter in my hand. I couldn't wait to tell her the good news.

CHAPTER 32
The Fine Print

"I remember this dress." Rick's finger trailed the row of buttons down my back, from my neck to the base of my spine.

"You couldn't possibly. It was designed just last year." I glanced over my shoulder at him, oddly nervous. We were in our bedroom, in the house that used to be mine but was now ours. Although we'd spent every night together since we'd returned from the West Coast, somehow this was different. Our first night as husband and wife.

"Let me see the tag." His fingers worked button after button, brushing his knuckles along my back and leaving a trail of heat in their wake. "Ah, here it is. Made with recycled vintage lace."

"Are you suggesting that by some miracle, the lace of my original wedding gown from the 1700s ended up on the wedding dress I'm wearing today?"

"I am not suggesting it, *mi cielo*. I know for sure. I remember."

I pivoted in his arms and reached up to work the knot from his bow tie. "I picked the right one then," I mumbled. The tie came loose in my fingers and I started in on his shirt buttons.

"Are you nervous?" He wrapped my hands in his, stopping my progress.

"Why would I be?"

"I do not know the why of it. Your heart beats faster, and I sense a wisp of fear in you."

I laughed through my nose. "I guess the downfall of sharing a metaphysical connection with you is that it will be hard to keep a secret."

"Yes. So, tell me why you are afraid."

"I have a wedding gift for you, but I'm not sure what you'll think of it."

He frowned at me. "I thought we agreed not to exchange gifts."

"We did."

Rick had wanted to buy me a vacation home as a gift, but it seemed too extravagant given my employment status at the time, not to mention I couldn't give him a suitable gift in return. "This isn't that type of gift. It's something I made for you, before you remembered me. Something I made just in case."

He took a step back and spread his hands. "Show me this gift."

I crossed the room to my dresser and dug in my underwear drawer until I found a box. I'd wrapped it in silver paper and tied it with an orchid-colored bow that matched our wedding colors.

"It's okay if you don't like it. We don't have to ever use them."

He stripped off his jacket and dress shirt and laid them across the chair before taking the box from me. He judged its weight in his hand as if trying to guess what it was, and then gave me a wicked half smile before starting in on the bow.

"It's funny," I said, while he worked on the knot, "facing death made me cherish life. My mother has a different sort of life in her place guarding the door to the underworld. She's powerful, but I think she's also lonely."

He tore off the wrapping paper, exposing the white box underneath and worked his fingers under the lid.

"I like being alive. Our life is risky. Our marriage is risky. Sometimes bad things are going to happen. But I think it's worth it," I said.

"Candles?" He looked at the six dark purple tapers in his hand in confusion.

"While I still had Tabetha's grimoire and her power, I reproduced her humanity spell."

"You want me to become human again?"

"Only for a night, now and then."

He stared at the candles, eyebrows converging over his nose. All at once, his face went slack. "You want to try for a baby?" His voice was barely a whisper.

"It doesn't have to be tonight or even this year. I just made them to give us options."

"I thought we decided having a human child would be too dangerous, too fragile."

"That's the thing. We don't know for sure he or she would be human entirely, do we? I have your blood in my veins." I tangled my fingers together. "Honestly, we don't even know if it will work. So much of our relationship is taking risks. Trying things. Trusting fate. Playing the odds."

"There are six in here."

"In for a penny, in for a pound." I giggled nervously.

Rick turned his back on me and walked to the bed. I couldn't see what he was doing, but I heard the little drawer in the bedside table open. The box rattled. The drawer shut again. Well, he knew they existed. We could keep them there and someday in the future, maybe Rick would come around to the idea.

He turned back to me, giving me a clear view of the table. One of the candles rose from a brass holder I'd kept in the drawer.

"Will you do the honors?" he said, motioning toward the wick. "I don't want to have to waste time retrieving a lighter from the kitchen."

My heart leaped. With a strong breath of air, I ignited the wick.

He strode toward me, a cloud of desire darkening his irises. "Do we have to wait until it burns all the way down?"

"Hell no." I reached for his belt and pulled it from his pants. "We just have to still be doing it when it gets there."

"Good." He captured my face in his hands and melded his mouth to mine. I returned the kiss with long strokes of my tongue, the feel of his hands unbuttoning the last of my dress driving me mad with desire. My dress fell from my shoulders and pooled around my ankles, leaving me in a white lace bra set and garters. When I moved to kick off my heels, he grabbed my hip.

"Leave them on," he said with a grin.

I shook my head. "My feet hurt from dancing all night."

"So let's get you off them." In one smooth jerk, my panties went flying in pieces across the room. He wrapped his hands around my waist and lifted me until I was perched on top of the dresser with his chest between my knees.

"Better?" he whispered. Soft, warm kisses trailed down from my navel.

"Not quite yet," I whispered. I leaned back and spread my knees wider.

His lips grazed my inner thigh and kept moving south.

"Much better," I mumbled.

* * * * *

It was almost sunrise when I finally closed my eyes, soaking up the blissful, sleepy state Rick left me in. The weight of his body shifted above me, and his teeth grazed my neck.

"Wake up, *mi cielo*," he whispered into my ear. "The candle isn't finished and neither am I."

His teeth struck my jugular, and the rhythm of his swallowing revived me. I repositioned myself and bit the wrist he offered. As his blood flowed over my tongue, I bucked under him from the taste of it, and he responded in kind, entering me again.

I watched the wax drip languidly down the taper of my making and thought, *Take your time. I'm not going anywhere.*

CHAPTER 33
Twenty-Eight Seconds

Twenty-two months later...

I slipped inside through the door from the garage, closing it quietly behind me. Rick looked up from his seat at the island, a parenting magazine open on the counter. He smiled at me, and I noticed he had what looked like pureed peas in his hair. At least I hoped it was pureed peas.

"How was work?" he whispered.

"Good. Normal." I pointed at the ceiling.

"Napping," he said.

Our son, Lucas, was a miracle and, so far, brilliantly normal. A blessing in every way. I loved him with everything in me, but he rarely slept and time alone with Rick had become an unusual privilege.

"Hurry," I said, stripping off my scrubs. I was naked in less than thirty seconds.

Rick was slower to undress.

"What's wrong?"

"Tired."

"You're never tired!" I said, helping him with his shirt.

He shrugged, slightly offended.

"What is this? Applesauce?" I asked as I removed his pants.

"New organic chicken pot pie recipe," he said.

I smelled it. The scent was intolerable, like a cross between vomit and retirement home. "You did a good job. Smells yummy."

He pursed his lips at me. "I am wearing most of it. He thinks it is funny to throw it."

"Did you have Poe—?"

"Do the open-up-baby-birdie trick? Yes. It didn't work. He's getting too smart for that."

"I'm sure he'll be fine." I knocked him to the carpet and straddled his hips. We didn't bother with foreplay. I joined with him and got busy.

"You have blood in your hair," he said with concern.

"Not mine. Gunshot wound."

"Good."

He rolled me onto my back. The carpet burned my skin but I didn't complain. I pulled him closer.

Whaa. Whaaaaa.

We stopped, ears trained on the ceiling. The crying stopped.

"Hurry. Hurry," I said.

He obeyed. It was magical... for twenty-eight seconds.

Whaaa. Whaaaa, whaaaa! Ma ma. Ma ma.

I rolled Rick over and pointed at the ceiling. "Did he?"

"I think he did." Rick smiled.

Leaping off my husband, I tossed on my scrubs and took the stairs two by two. Lucas's room was right next to ours. We'd painted the walls to look like a forest, and Rick had built his crib on a wide base with branches like a tree house.

My son had pulled himself up on his crib rail. He smiled his two-toothed smile and blinked massive blue eyes at me when I walked into his room.

"Ma ma ma," he said.

"Where's my little monkey?" I ran to his crib and lifted him out to blow raspberries on his stomach. Lucas burst into belly laughs.

I glanced back at Rick, who leaned in the doorway, beaming.

"I think he grew while I was at work," I said, holding Lucas above my head and lowering him for loud smacking kisses that made him squeal.

"He grows every day."

"You don't think he's growing too much, do you?"

"The doctor says he's completely normal."

"Yes, but do you think... you know... that he is? Completely normal."

Rick shrugged. "What does normal mean anyway?"

"Right. As long as he's healthy." I sat Lucas on my hip and brought him over to Rick. "He's so beautiful." I kissed Rick on the cheek.

"You're a natural at this," Rick said, stroking back his son's blond hair.

"I'm glad you think so."

Rick waved at Lucas, opening and closing his fingers, and Lucas waved back, opening and closing his chubby hand.

"I'm *glad* you think so," I repeated more slowly.

"Why are you saying the words like that?" he asked, getting greedy and pulling Lucas into his arms.

"Because we're going to have another one."

Rick's face went stony, and I placed my hands under Lucas, afraid he might slip from my catatonic husband's grip.

"Another one?"

"We did do the candle thing again," I reminded him. I rearranged my scrubs to reveal the small rounded mound of my lower belly. "I'm about ten weeks, I think."

Rick said nothing. He blinked at me. He wasn't breathing. I reached out and shook his shoulder. "Are you okay? Is this... is this okay?" I whispered it, although I'm not sure why. Lucas could still hear me and was much too young to understand what I was saying.

A slow, broad smile bloomed across Rick's face. "It is more than okay, Grateful. Two for two. Do you think we'll end up with six?"

I raised my eyebrows. "Maybe. More if we have twins."

His face paled. "Is that possible?"

I threaded my fingers into his. "Who knows? But let's just start with two."

He kissed me on the cheek and allowed me to lead him from the room. "We should call your father."

"He's coming tonight to babysit while we patrol. We'll tell him then," I said. "He's going to flip."

"*Mi ceilo?*" Rick stopped me in the hall.

"Yeah?"

He pulled Lucas and me into a hug, kissing me on the mouth. "I love you. I love our family." He placed his hand on my lower belly.

"I love you too. I always have, and I always will."

He touched his forehead to mine.

I was his witch and he was my caretaker, and we were happy forever after.

EPILOGUE

Lucas sat up in his crib and whimpered quietly. He was supposed to be sleeping, but he wasn't tired at all. In fact, he was rarely tired. Although he could tolerate lying in his crib sometimes, he didn't need as much sleep as the adults in his life seemed to think he needed. Tonight, the room was dark, except for the moon that shown through the branches of the tree outside his window. That was the problem. The branches, along with the wind, cast strange shadows across his floor. He was afraid.

He'd made up his mind that *alone* was not what he wanted to be at the moment and took a deep breath, intending to cry. He stopped when a dark-haired woman walked out of the shadows and placed her finger over her lips.

"Shhh. Hello, Lucas," she said. She raised one hand, opening and closing her fingers.

Lucas opened and closed his hand too.

"Do you know who I am?" The woman reached inside his crib and pulled him into her arms. "I'm your grandma."

Grandma. That was a funny word. "Me ma," he repeated.

"Yes. Grandma. Now, I noticed you were scared, so I came." She walked him over to the window and pointed outside. "Don't be afraid of the wind. I am in the wind, and I will never blow you down." She pointed at the tree. "Don't be afraid of the tree. I live in the trees. If you are ever afraid, run straight to a tree, and I will protect you. Do you want to see what I can make the trees do?"

Lucas blinked at her and she smiled in response. With a wave of her hand, the branches of the tree began to grow and change, sprouting and blooming. The branches formed symbols.

"That's your name," she said. "That spells Lucas." She kissed him on the cheek. "You are a darling, aren't you?"

She walked him back to the center of the room and sat down with him on the rug. "Don't be afraid of the dark. I am in the dark, and I will always watch over you." She held out her hands and lit a tiny green ball of fire, then a blue, and a red, and juggled them between her palms.

Lucas laughed. He liked the grandma woman. One of the balls popped out of its orbit and landed on his nose. Only, it wasn't fire when it hit his skin but a raindrop. Lucas laughed even louder.

"Shhh," Grandma said. "We can't wake your parents. They need their sleep."

Lucas quieted down.

"I brought you someone to play with." She beckoned with her finger and a dog crept from the shadow in the corner. "This is Bosco. He's big but he will never hurt you."

Bosco lowered his nose to sniff Lucas, who laughed and pulled Bosco's ears. The big black hound licked the boy's cheek and lay down, curling himself behind the boy's back.

"There. See now. That's nice." Grandma scratched behind Bosco's ears and kissed Lucas on the forehead. With a snap of her fingers, Bosco transformed into a smaller stuffed version of himself. "Bosco will stay with you when I can't. He'll watch over you and tell me if you need me. See, there's never been a little boy like you before. Even I am not sure what the future holds for you. But no matter. Your grandma will be there for you, no matter what."

Lucas hugged the stuffed dog around the neck and rubbed its velvet ears between his fingers. Grandma picked him up and put him and the stuffed dog back into the crib.

"I once told your mother she was my favorite." She tapped Lucas on the nose. "Not anymore." She backed away, toward the shadow in the corner of his room. "I must go now, but I'll be back. I'll keep you safe. I promise."

And she did. Forevermore.

COMING SOON

Don't miss the next installment, LOGAN a Knight World novel. Sign up to learn more at http://bit.ly/KnowJackNews .

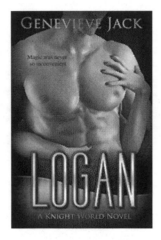

Logan Valentine hates witches. After being drugged and tortured by one in the past, he's sworn off magical types for good. Even when a certain redheaded witch plays the starring role in his hottest dreams, he vows to focus on running his restaurant and leading a normal human life.

Polina Innes thinks humans belong in the same category as dogs or pigs. The centuries old witch abhors cross-species romance and hates herself for fantasizing about the blond human she met helping a fellow witch last year. As her thoughts border on obsession, she becomes desperate to cure herself of her rogue desires using any means possible.

When Polina finds a love potion guaranteed to connect her with her soulmate, she's sure it's the answer to wiping Logan from her mind for good. Only, her plan backfires. One sip leads her to his door and unleashes an unwanted attraction that becomes increasingly impossible to deny.

ABOUT THE AUTHOR

Genevieve Jack grew up in a suburb of Chicago and attended a high school rumored to be haunted. She loves old cemeteries and enjoys a good ghost tour. Genevieve specializes in original, cross-genre stories with surprising twists. She lives in central Illinois with her husband, two children, and a Brittany named Riptide who holds down her feet while she writes.

Sign up to learn about new releases at http://bit.ly/KnowJackNews.

Visit Genevieve at:
   http://www.GenevieveJack.com
   https://twitter.com/Genevieve_Jack
   https://www.facebook.com/AuthorGenevieveJack

ACKNOWLEDGEMENTS

Mother May I would not have been possible without the help of a few individuals who gave of their time and experience.

To my husband, thank you for your support and encouragement. I appreciate all those times you handled the real world while I was building a fantasy one.

Special thanks to Laurie Larsen, RT Wolfe, and Katy Lewis for their priceless advice on the manuscript.

Finally, huge hugs to Hollie Westring, the fabulous editor who helps me bring it all together in the end.

Made in the USA
Middletown, DE
20 April 2021